THE BASEBALL ADVENTURE OF JACKIE MITCHELL,

GIRL PITCHER VS. BABE RUTH

BY **JEAN L. S. PATRICK**
ADAPTED BY **EMMA CARLSON BERNE**
ILLUSTRATED BY **TED HAMMOND** AND **RICHARD PIMENTEL CARBAJAL**

Graphic Universe™ · Minneapolis · New York

INTRODUCTION

WOMEN HAVE BEEN PLAYING BASEBALL—NOT SOFTBALL—FOR MORE THAN 100 YEARS. VASSAR COLLEGE FORMED THE FIRST WOMEN'S TEAMS IN 1866. BACK THEN, A BATTER HAD TO PICK UP HER LONG, HEAVY SKIRT AND DRAPE IT OVER HER ARM BEFORE SHE COULD RUN TO FIRST BASE.

FROM THE 1890S THROUGH THE 1930S, THOUSANDS OF WOMEN PLAYED ON WOMEN'S BASEBALL TEAMS. THE PLAYERS WORE BLOOMERS—LOOSE, KNEE-LENGTH SHORTS—AND CAME TO BE CALLED BLOOMER GIRLS. OTHER WOMEN, SUCH AS LIZZIE MURPHY AND BABE DIDRIKSON, PLAYED ON MEN'S MAJOR-LEAGUE TEAMS DURING PRESEASON. OR THEY APPEARED IN EXHIBITION GAMES THAT WERE JUST FOR SHOW.

AT THAT TIME, MAJOR-LEAGUE TEAMS OFTEN PLAYED EXHIBITION GAMES WITH MINOR-LEAGUE OR SEMIPROFESSIONAL TEAMS DURING THE OFF-SEASON. THIS KEPT THE PLAYERS IN SHAPE. IT ALSO BROUGHT MAJOR-LEAGUE TEAMS INTO CITIES WHERE THEY DID NOT USUALLY PLAY, GIVING MORE OF THEIR FANS A CHANCE TO SEE THEM.

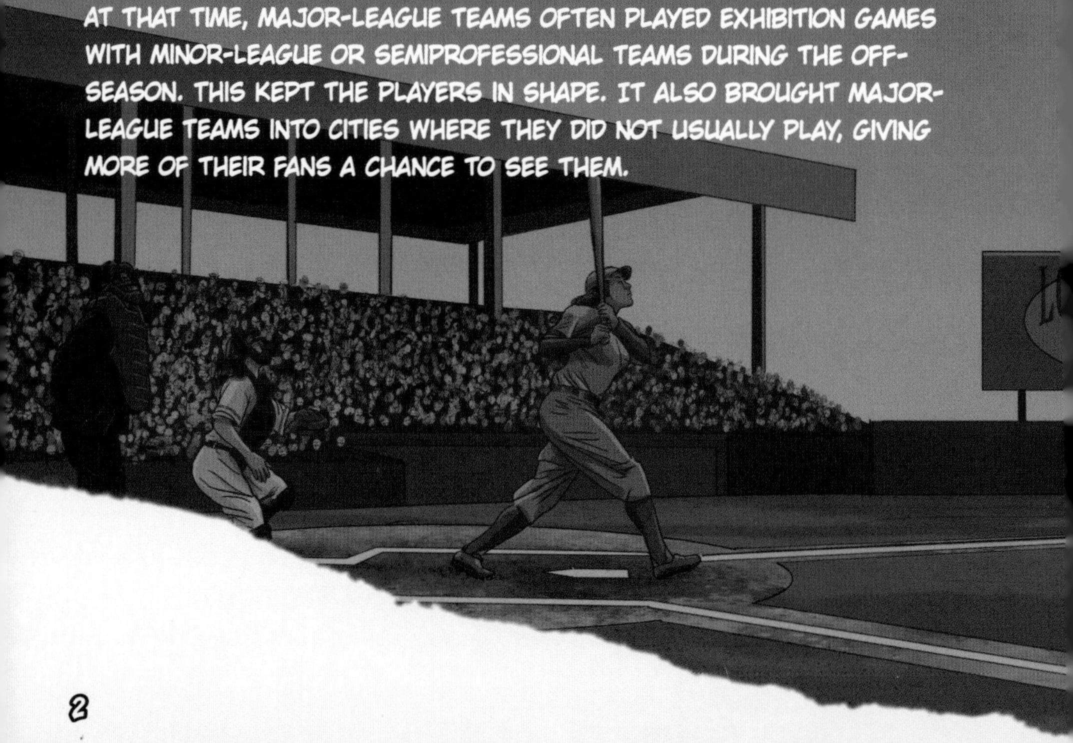

ONE OF THE MOST TALENTED PLAYERS WAS VIRNE BEATRICE "JACKIE" MITCHELL. WHEN SHE WAS A YOUNG GIRL, BASEBALL STAR DAZZY VANCE TAUGHT HER TO PITCH. IN 1930, AT THE AGE OF 16, JACKIE PLAYED ON THE ENGELETTES, A GIRLS' TEAM IN CHATTANOOGA, TENNESSEE. SHE OFTEN STRUCK OUT MEN FROM SEMIPROFESSIONAL TEAMS. A YEAR LATER, SHE TRAINED WITH FUTURE MAJOR-LEAGUE PLAYERS AT KID ELBERFELD'S FAMOUS BASEBALL SCHOOL IN ATLANTA, GEORGIA.

AT THIS TIME, JOE ENGEL WAS THE PRESIDENT OF THE CHATTANOOGA LOOKOUTS, A MINOR-LEAGUE MEN'S BASEBALL TEAM. HE KNEW JACKIE COULD BRING GREAT PUBLICITY TO THE LOOKOUTS. ON MARCH 25, 1931, JOE ENGEL ANNOUNCED THAT HE WOULD OFFER 17-YEAR-OLD JACKIE A PROFESSIONAL CONTRACT. BUT JACKIE COULDN'T SIGN. SHE WAS IN TEXAS, PLAYING IN A BASKETBALL TOURNAMENT.

ON SATURDAY, MARCH 28, JACKIE MITCHELL RETURNED TO CHATTANOOGA. BASEBALL WAS ON HER MIND.

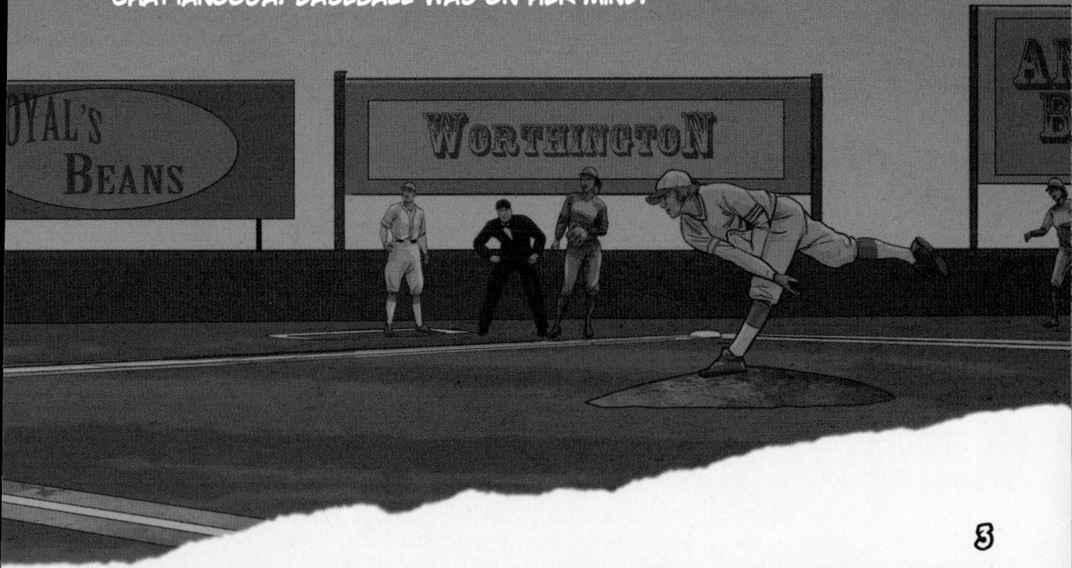
BEANS
WORTHINGTON

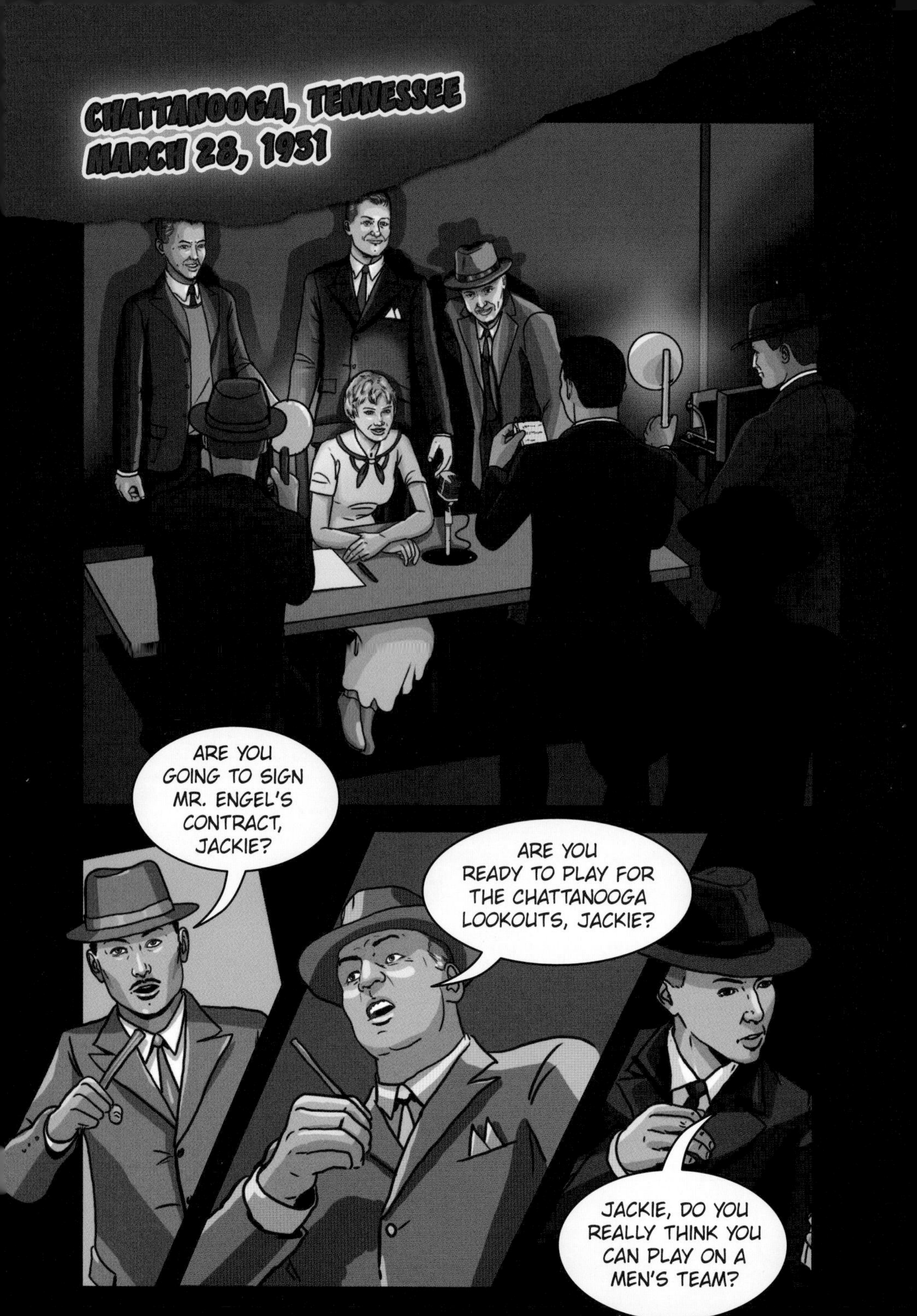
CHATTANOOGA, TENNESSEE
MARCH 28, 1931
ARE YOU GOING TO SIGN MR. ENGEL'S CONTRACT, JACKIE?
ARE YOU READY TO PLAY FOR THE CHATTANOOGA LOOKOUTS, JACKIE?
JACKIE, DO YOU REALLY THINK YOU CAN PLAY ON A MEN'S TEAM?

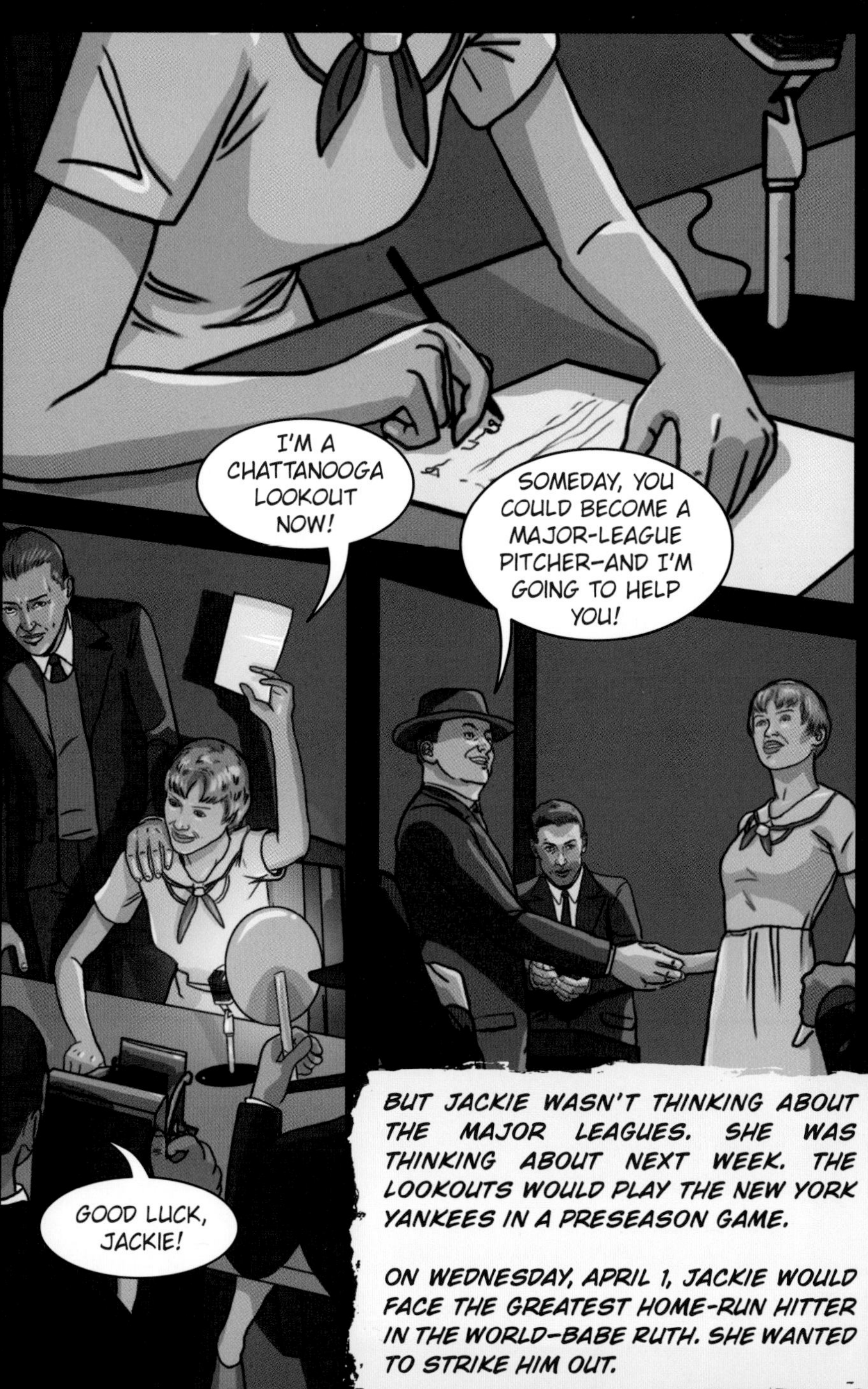
I'M A CHATTANOOGA LOOKOUT NOW!
SOMEDAY, YOU COULD BECOME A MAJOR-LEAGUE PITCHER—AND I'M GOING TO HELP YOU!
BUT JACKIE WASN'T THINKING ABOUT THE MAJOR LEAGUES. SHE WAS THINKING ABOUT NEXT WEEK. THE LOOKOUTS WOULD PLAY THE NEW YORK YANKEES IN A PRESEASON GAME.
ON WEDNESDAY, APRIL 1, JACKIE WOULD FACE THE GREATEST HOME-RUN HITTER IN THE WORLD—BABE RUTH. SHE WANTED TO STRIKE HIM OUT.
GOOD LUCK, JACKIE!

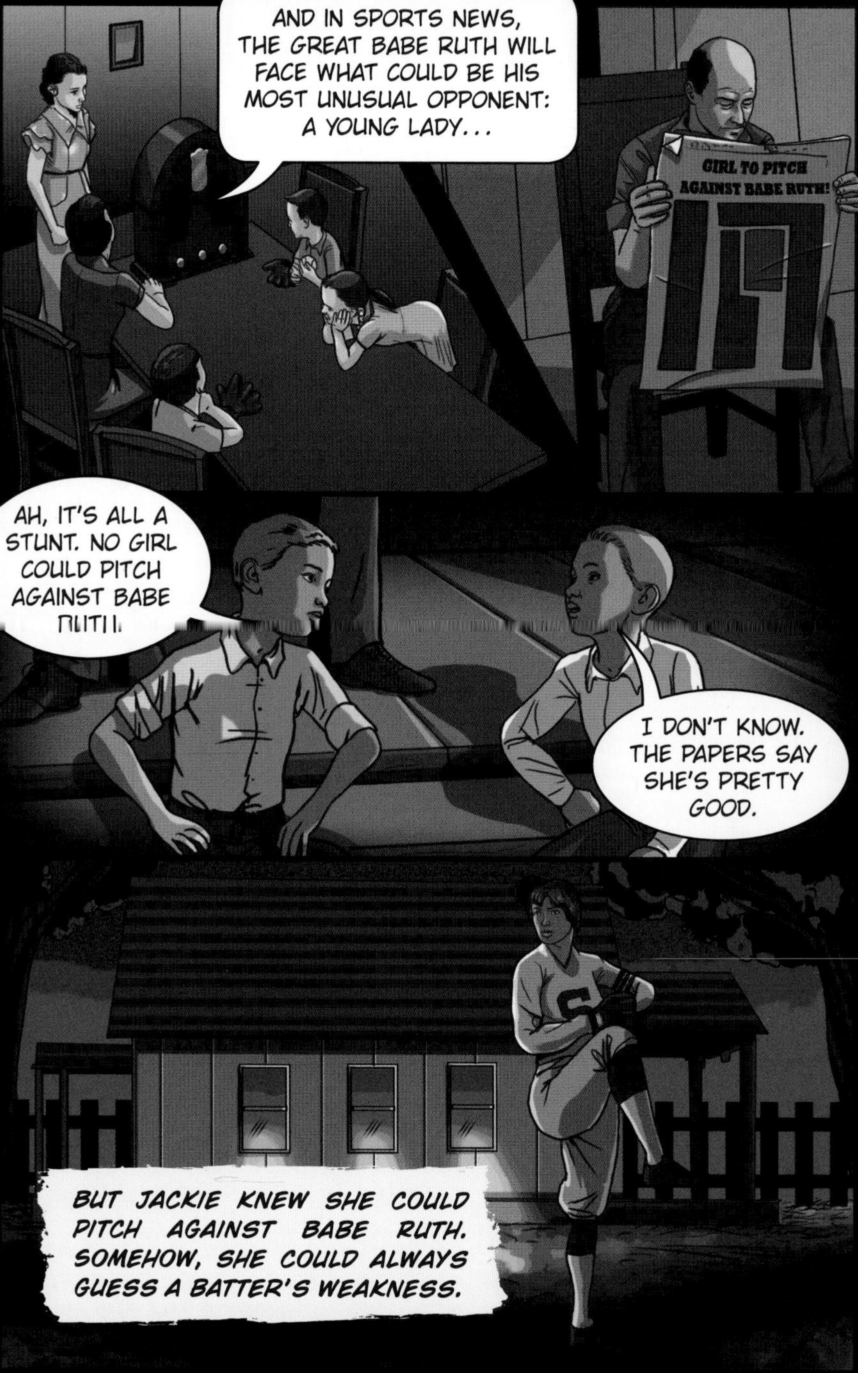
AND IN SPORTS NEWS, THE GREAT BABE RUTH WILL FACE WHAT COULD BE HIS MOST UNUSUAL OPPONENT: A YOUNG LADY...
GIRL TO PITCH AGAINST BABE RUTH!
AH, IT'S ALL A STUNT. NO GIRL COULD PITCH AGAINST BABE RUTH.
I DON'T KNOW. THE PAPERS SAY SHE'S PRETTY GOOD.
BUT JACKIE KNEW SHE COULD PITCH AGAINST BABE RUTH. SOMEHOW, SHE COULD ALWAYS GUESS A BATTER'S WEAKNESS.

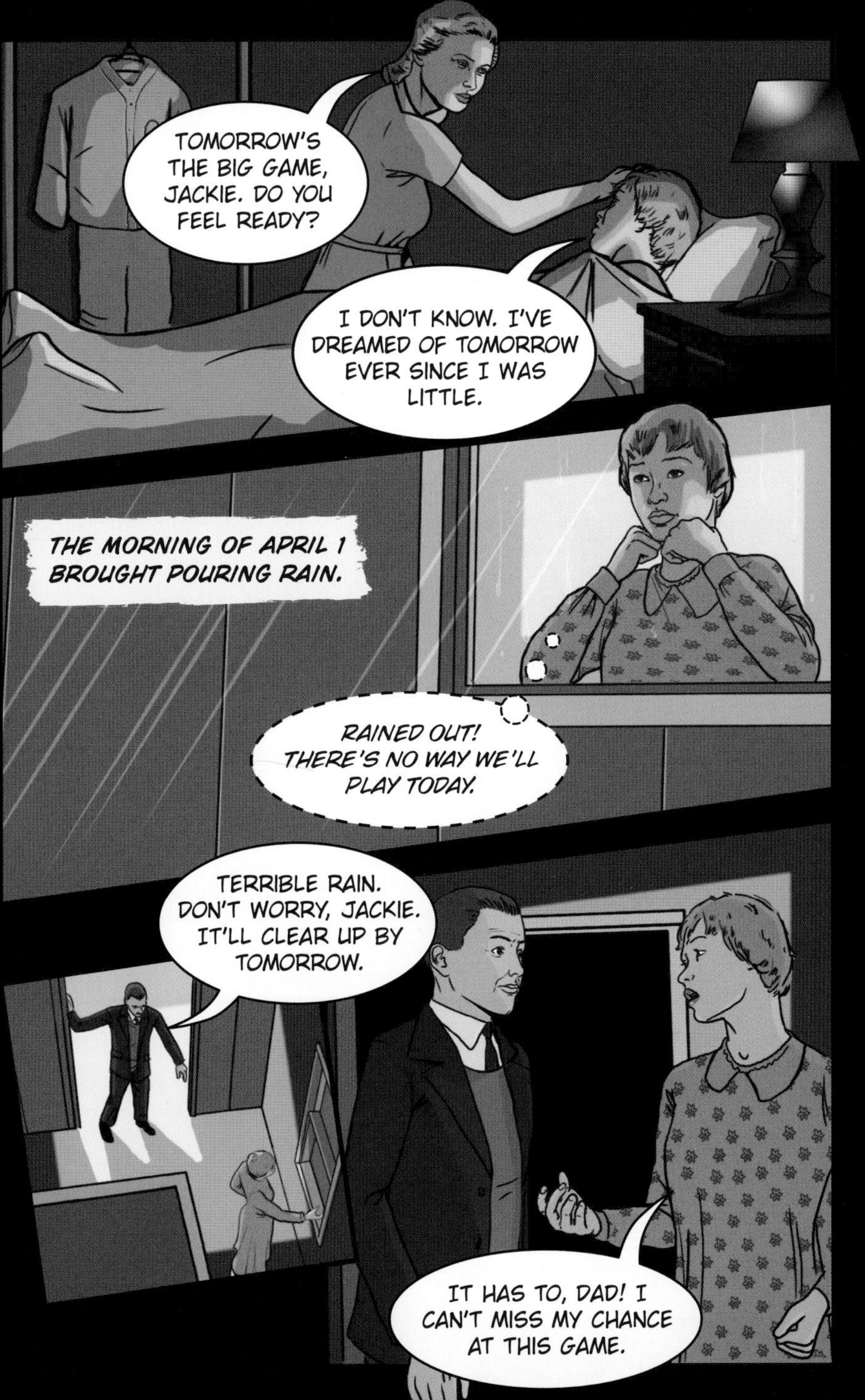
TOMORROW'S THE BIG GAME, JACKIE. DO YOU FEEL READY?
I DON'T KNOW. I'VE DREAMED OF TOMORROW EVER SINCE I WAS LITTLE.
THE MORNING OF APRIL 1 BROUGHT POURING RAIN.
RAINED OUT! THERE'S NO WAY WE'LL PLAY TODAY.
TERRIBLE RAIN. DON'T WORRY, JACKIE. IT'LL CLEAR UP BY TOMORROW.
IT HAS TO, DAD! I CAN'T MISS MY CHANCE AT THIS GAME.

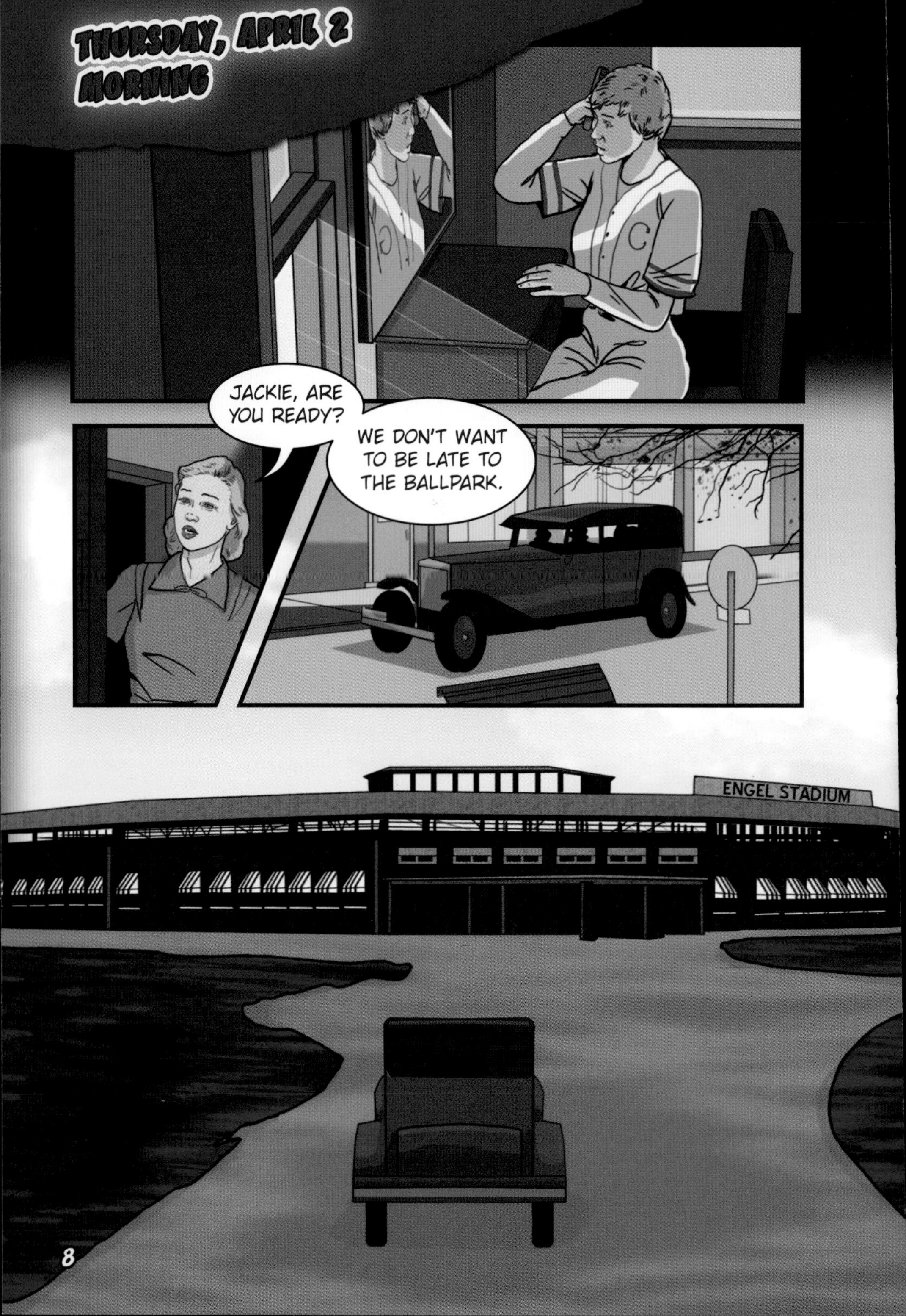
THURSDAY, APRIL 2
MORNING
JACKIE, ARE YOU READY?
WE DON'T WANT TO BE LATE TO THE BALLPARK.
ENGEL STADIUM

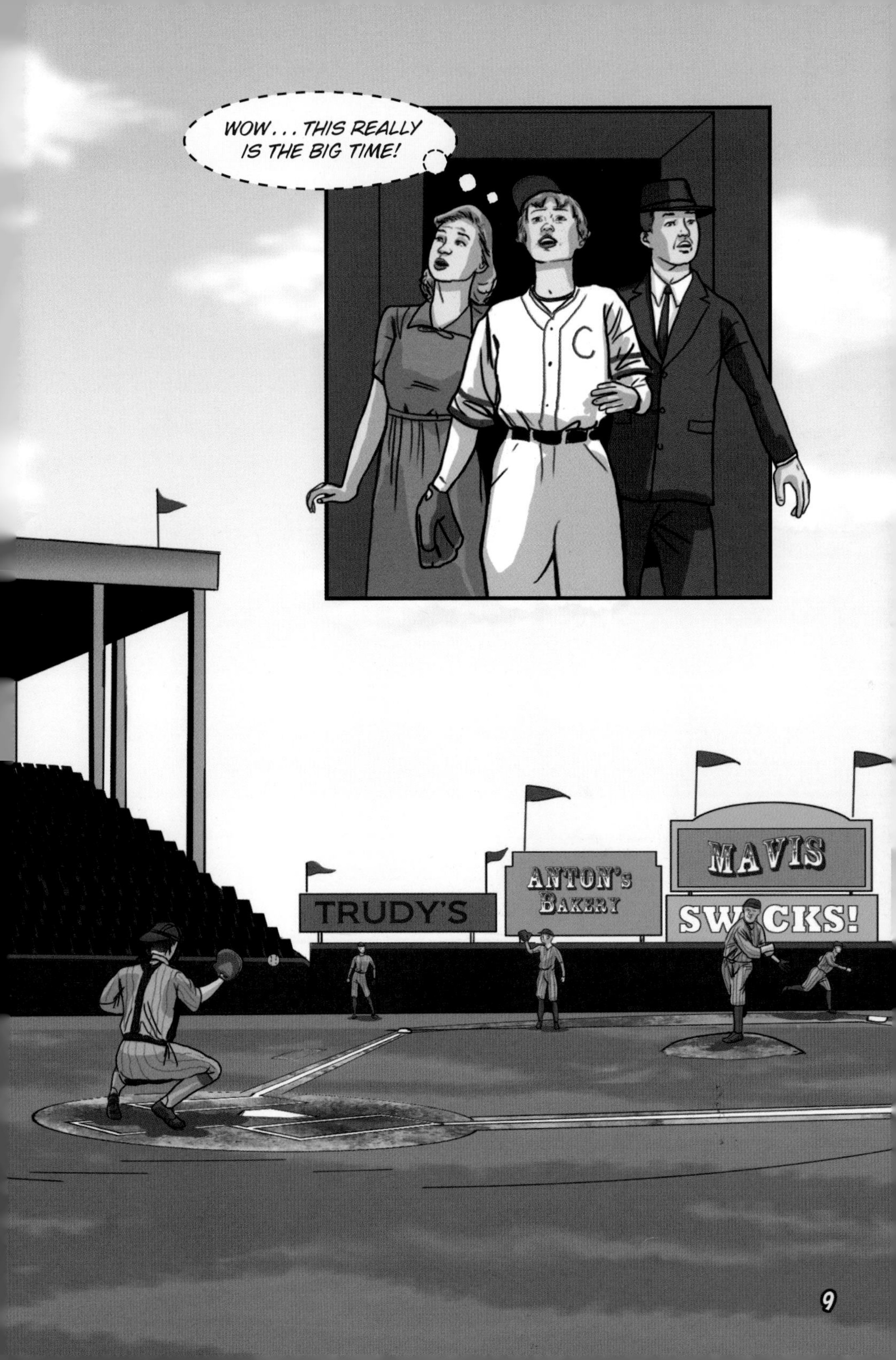
WOW... THIS REALLY IS THE BIG TIME!
TRUDY'S
ANTON's BAKERY
MAVIS

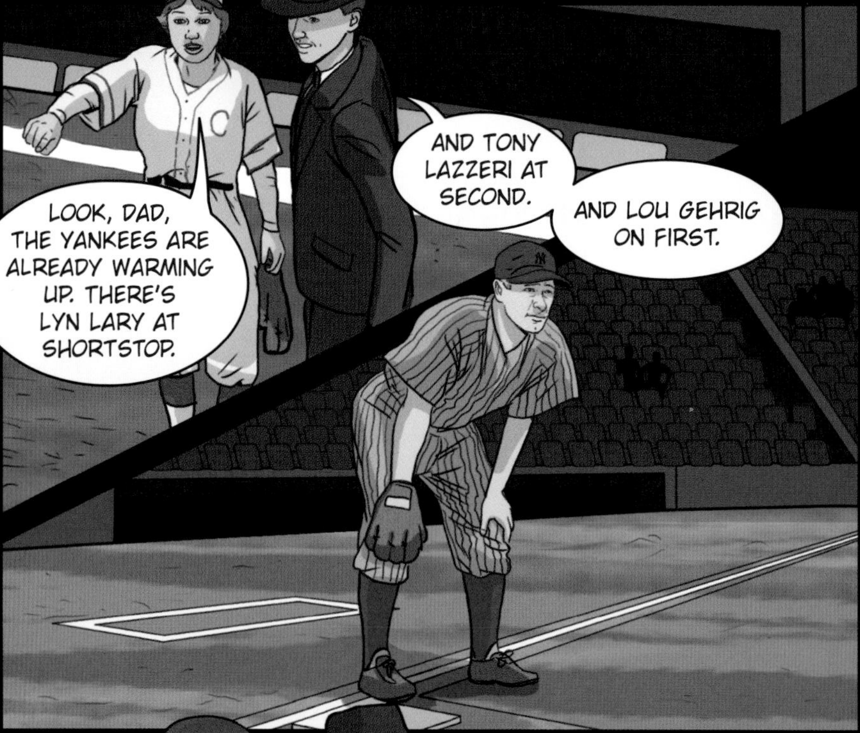
LOOK, DAD, THE YANKEES ARE ALREADY WARMING UP. THERE'S LYN LARY AT SHORTSTOP.
AND TONY LAZZERI AT SECOND.
AND LOU GEHRIG ON FIRST.

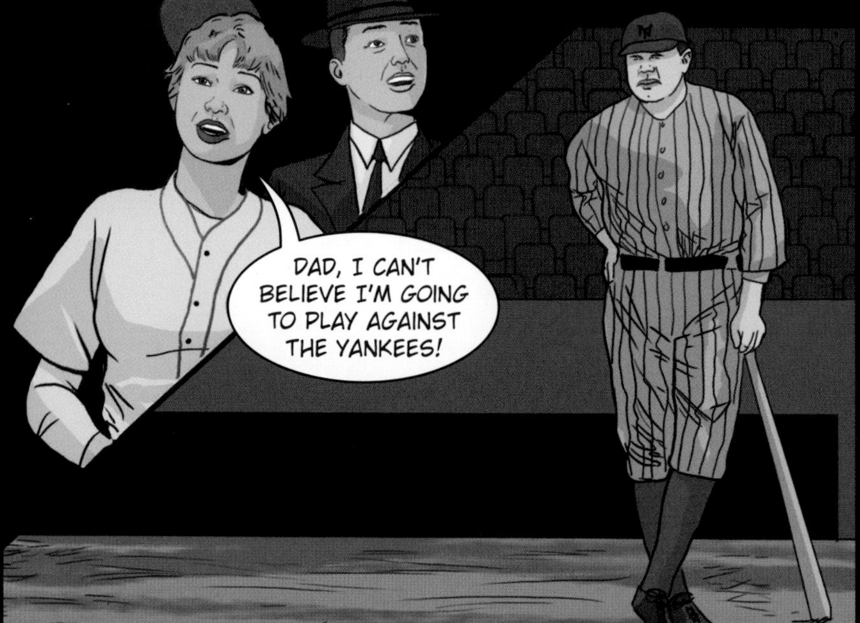
DAD, I CAN'T BELIEVE I'M GOING TO PLAY AGAINST THE YANKEES!

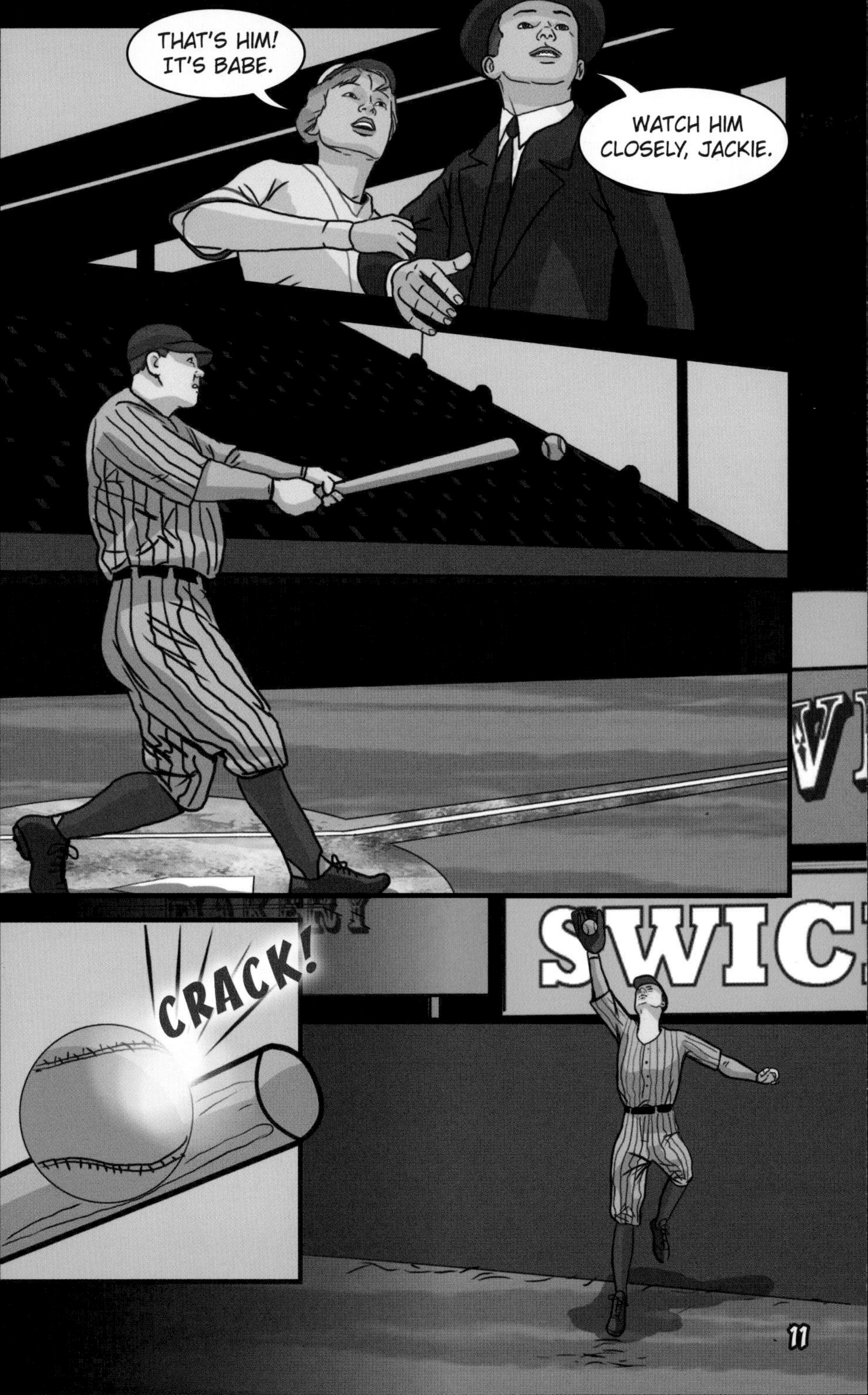

THAT'S HIM! IT'S BABE.
WATCH HIM CLOSELY, JACKIE.
CRACK!

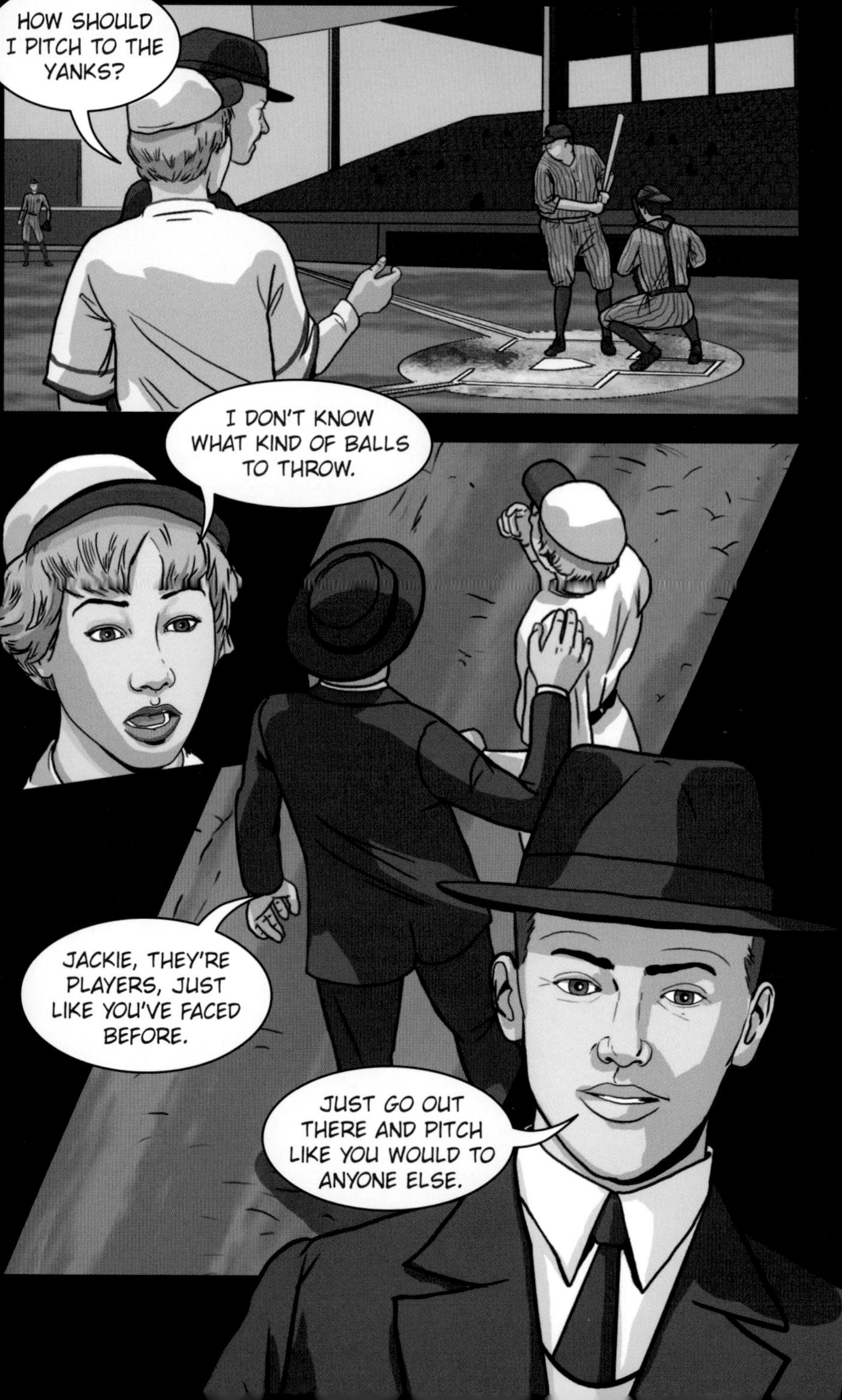
HOW SHOULD I PITCH TO THE YANKS?
I DON'T KNOW WHAT KIND OF BALLS TO THROW.
JACKIE, THEY'RE PLAYERS, JUST LIKE YOU'VE FACED BEFORE.
JUST GO OUT THERE AND PITCH LIKE YOU WOULD TO ANYONE ELSE.

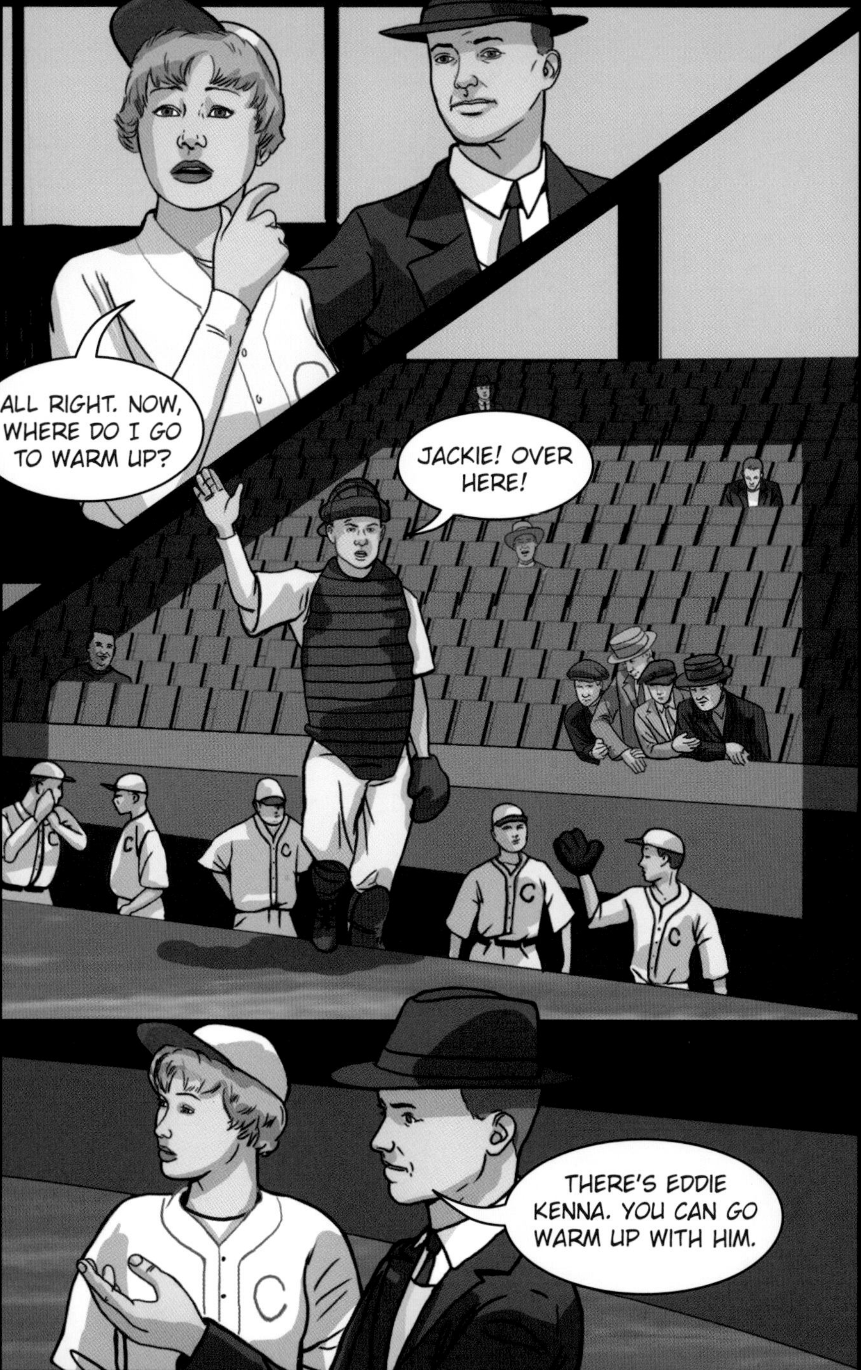
ALL RIGHT. NOW, WHERE DO I GO TO WARM UP?
JACKIE! OVER HERE!
THERE'S EDDIE KENNA. YOU CAN GO WARM UP WITH HIM.

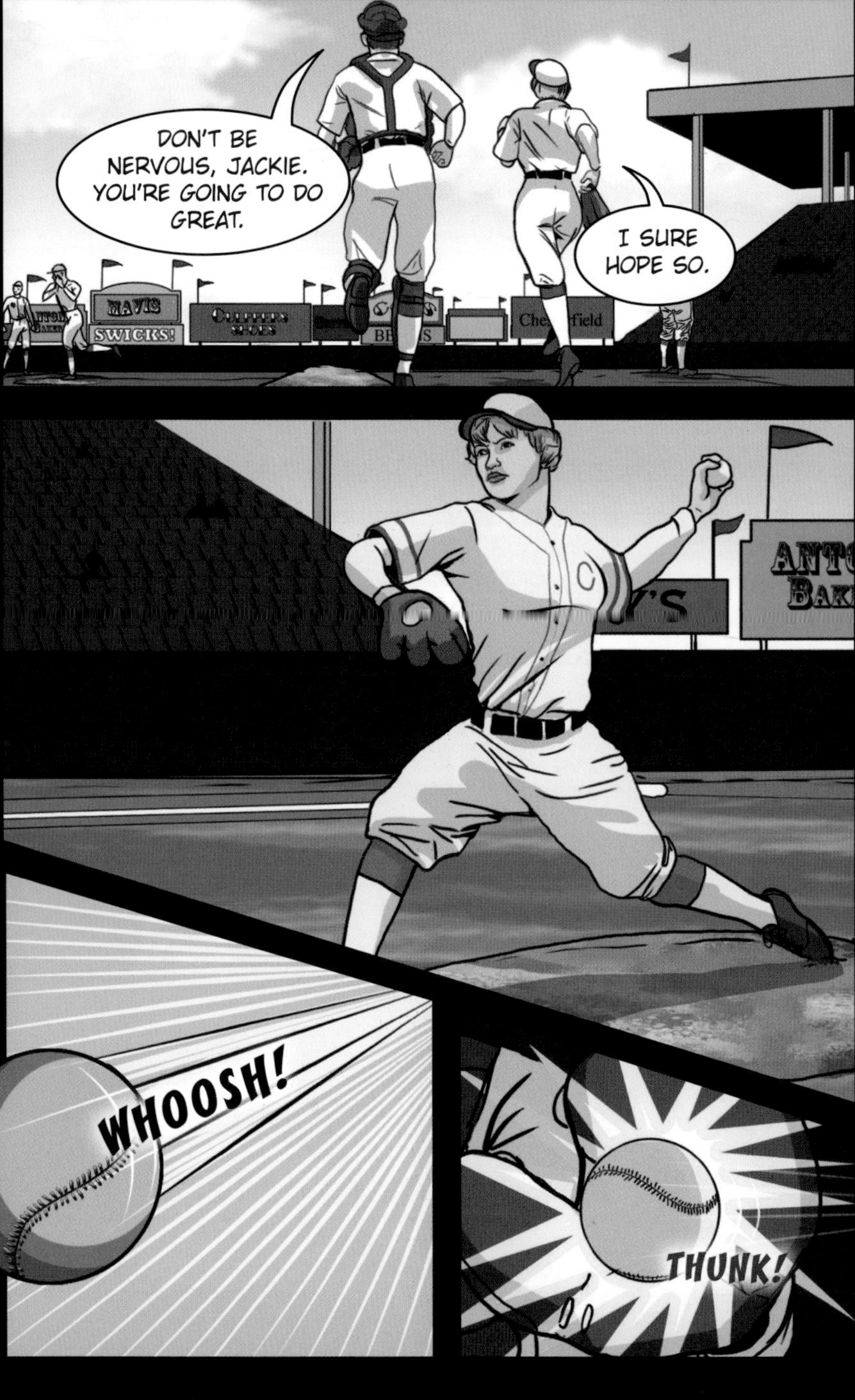
DON'T BE NERVOUS, JACKIE. YOU'RE GOING TO DO GREAT.
I SURE HOPE SO.
WHOOSH!
THUNK!

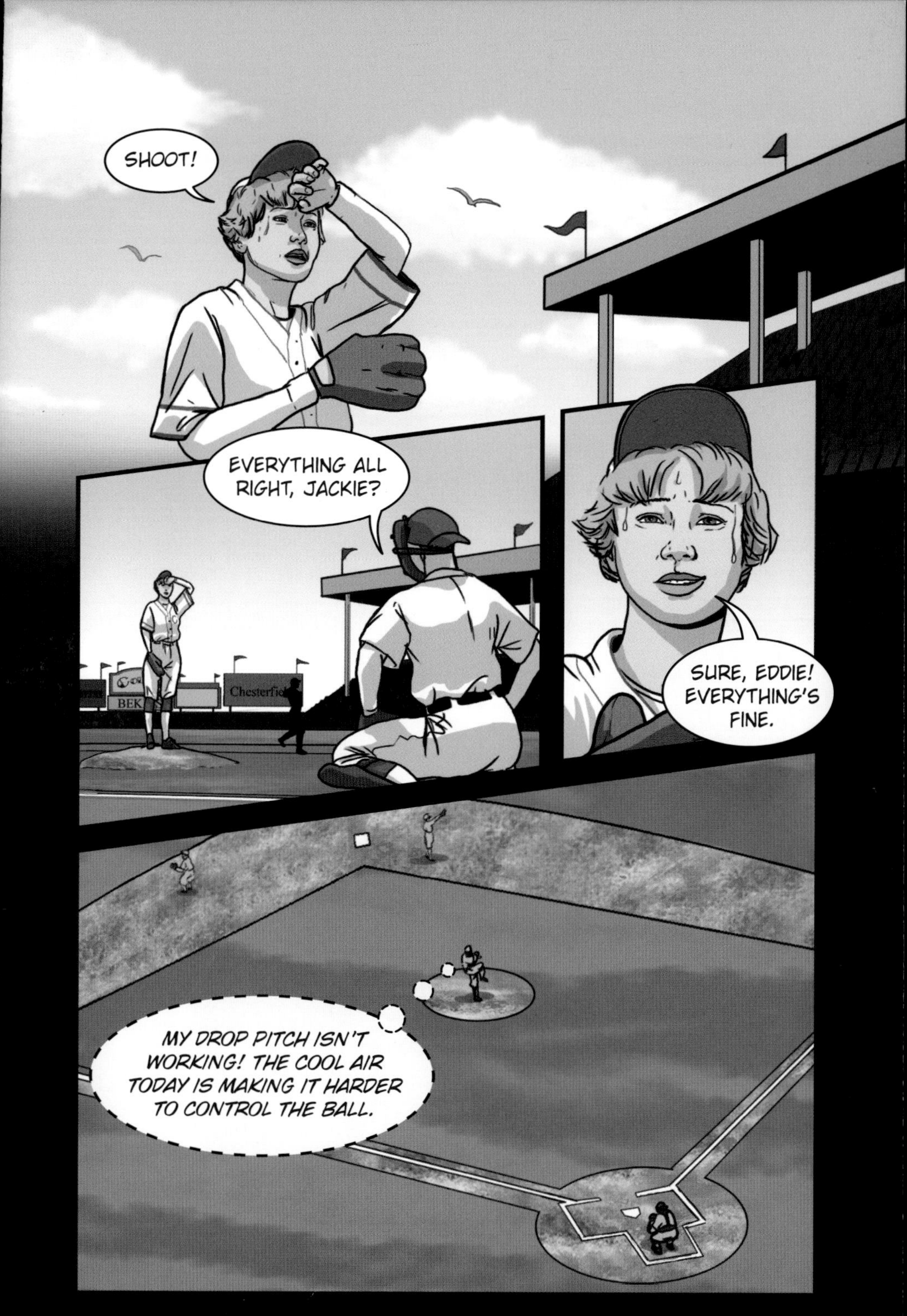
SHOOT!
EVERYTHING ALL RIGHT, JACKIE?
Chesterfie
BEK
SURE, EDDIE! EVERYTHING'S FINE.
MY DROP PITCH ISN'T WORKING! THE COOL AIR TODAY IS MAKING IT HARDER TO CONTROL THE BALL.

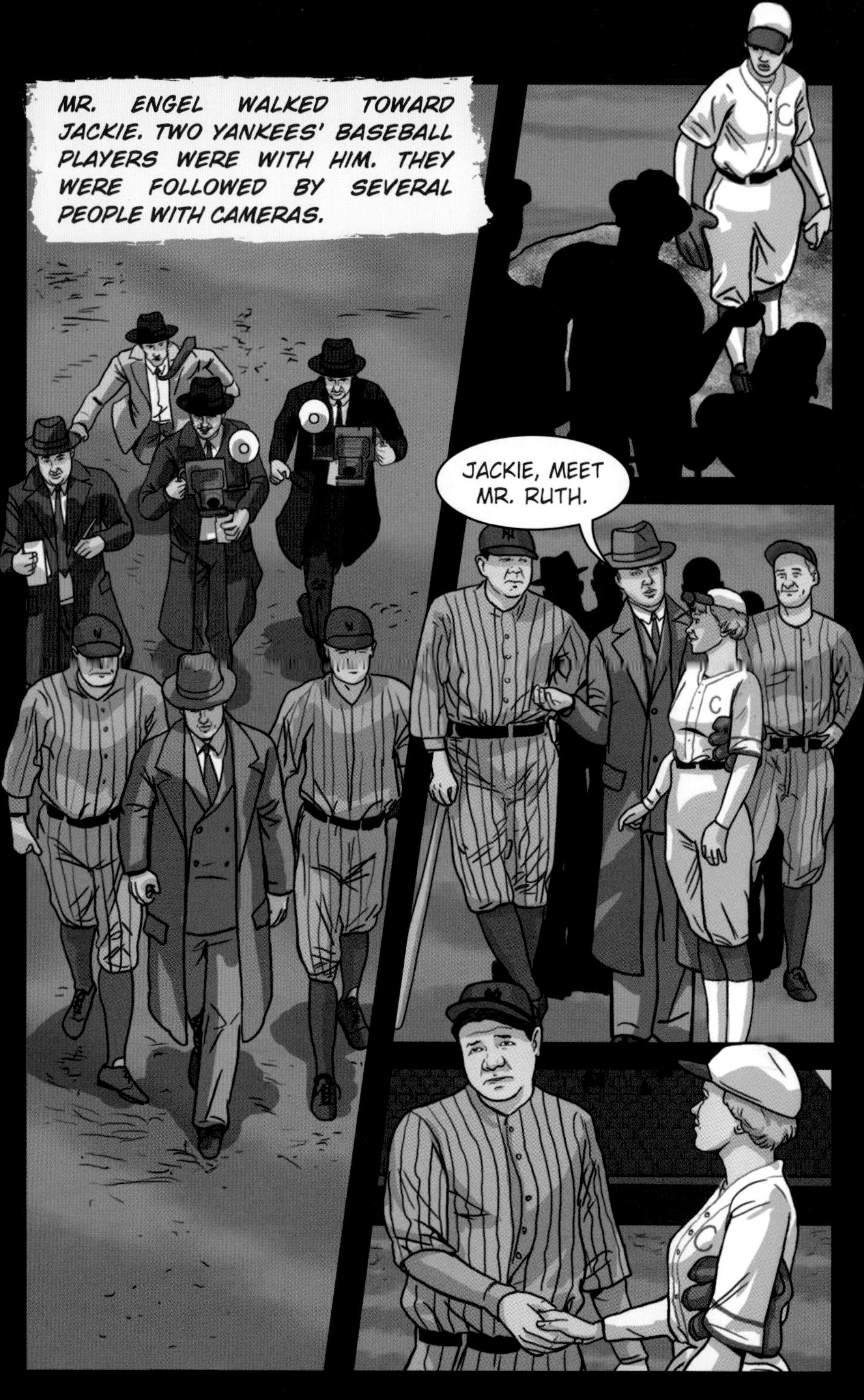
MR. ENGEL WALKED TOWARD JACKIE. TWO YANKEES' BASEBALL PLAYERS WERE WITH HIM. THEY WERE FOLLOWED BY SEVERAL PEOPLE WITH CAMERAS.
JACKIE, MEET MR. RUTH.

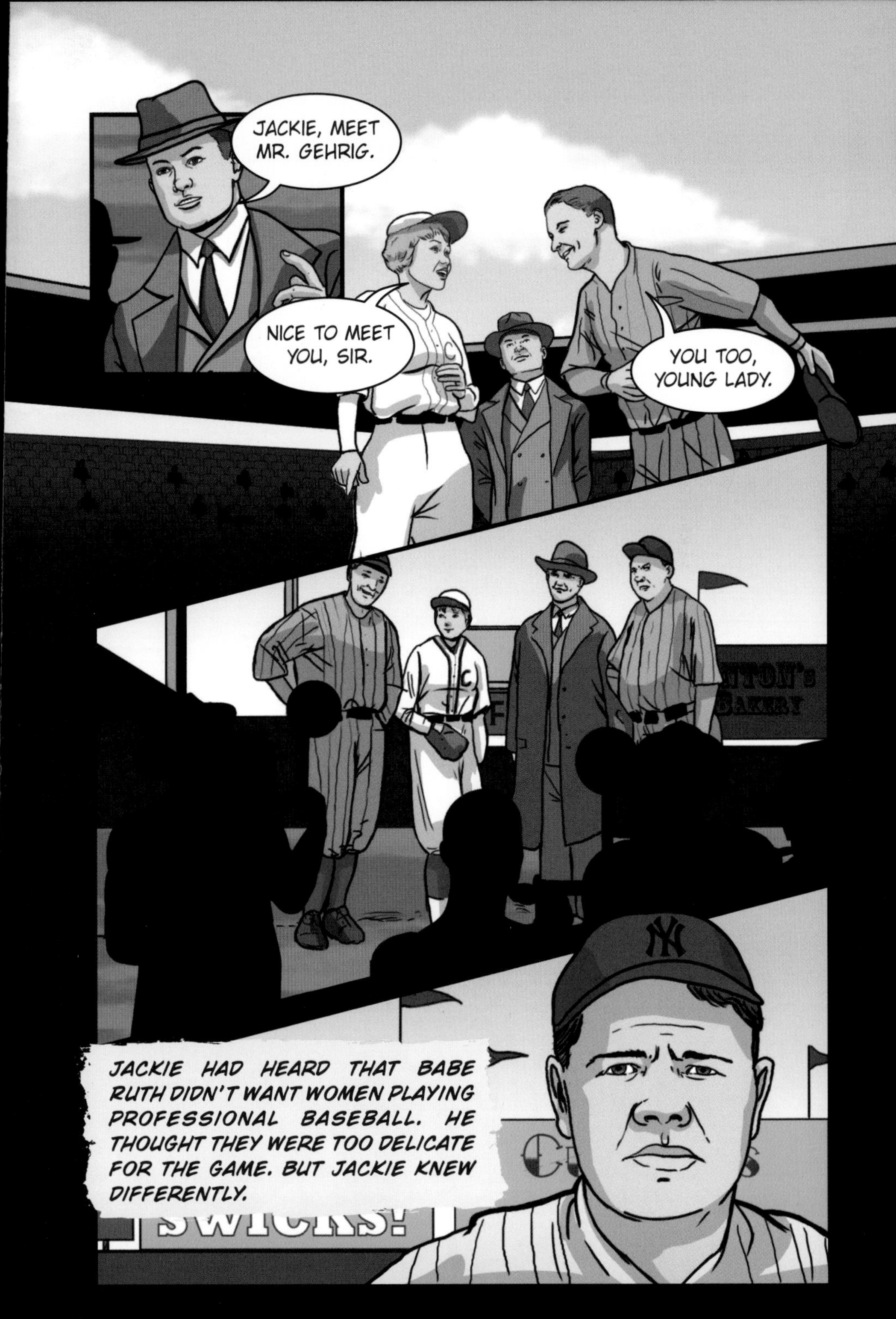
JACKIE, MEET MR. GEHRIG.
NICE TO MEET YOU, SIR.
YOU TOO, YOUNG LADY.
JACKIE HAD HEARD THAT BABE RUTH DIDN'T WANT WOMEN PLAYING PROFESSIONAL BASEBALL. HE THOUGHT THEY WERE TOO DELICATE FOR THE GAME. BUT JACKIE KNEW DIFFERENTLY.
SWICKS!

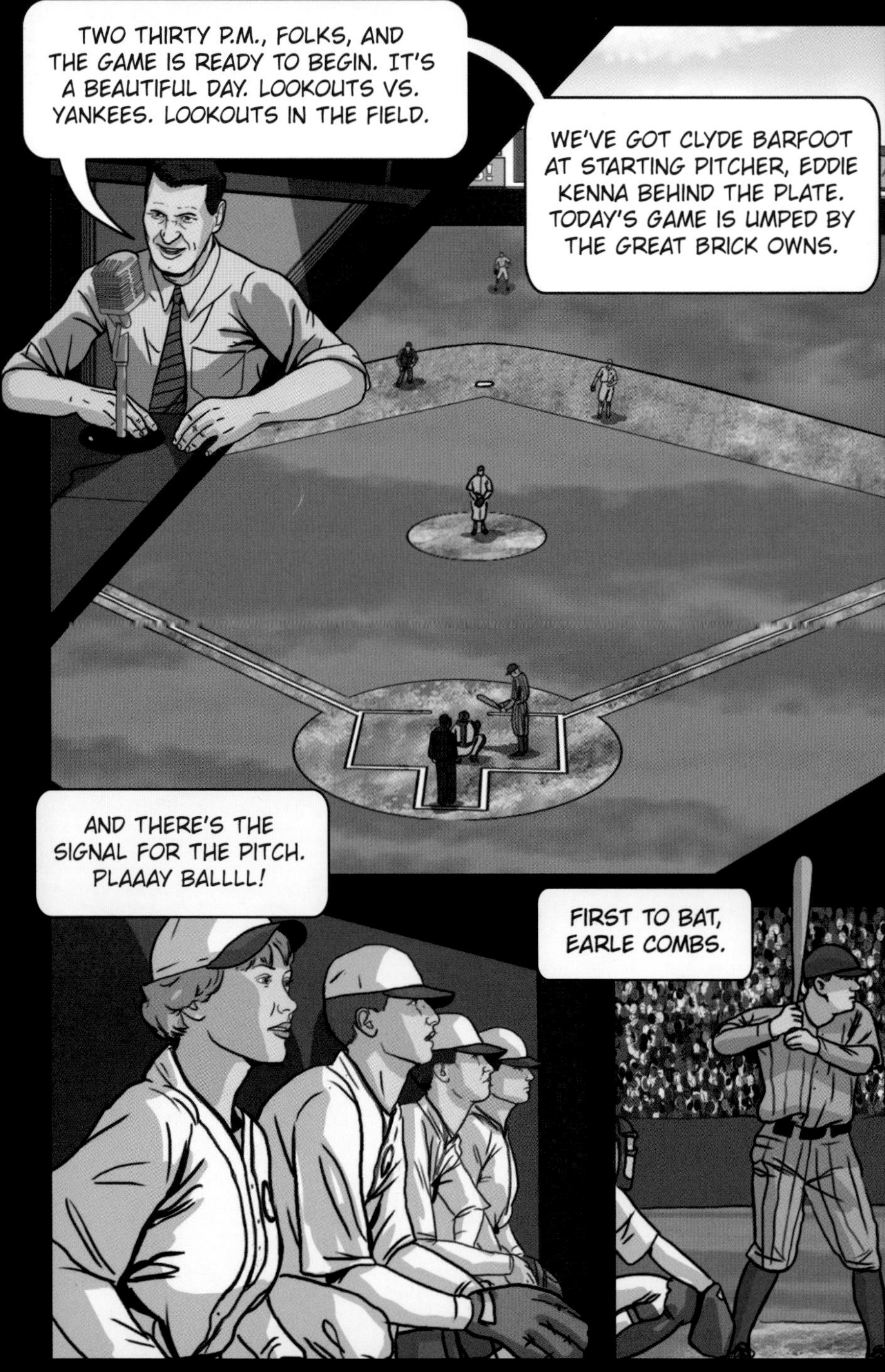
TWO THIRTY P.M., FOLKS, AND THE GAME IS READY TO BEGIN. IT'S A BEAUTIFUL DAY. LOOKOUTS VS. YANKEES. LOOKOUTS IN THE FIELD.
WE'VE GOT CLYDE BARFOOT AT STARTING PITCHER, EDDIE KENNA BEHIND THE PLATE. TODAY'S GAME IS UMPED BY THE GREAT BRICK OWNS.
AND THERE'S THE SIGNAL FOR THE PITCH. PLAAAY BALLLL!
FIRST TO BAT, EARLE COMBS.

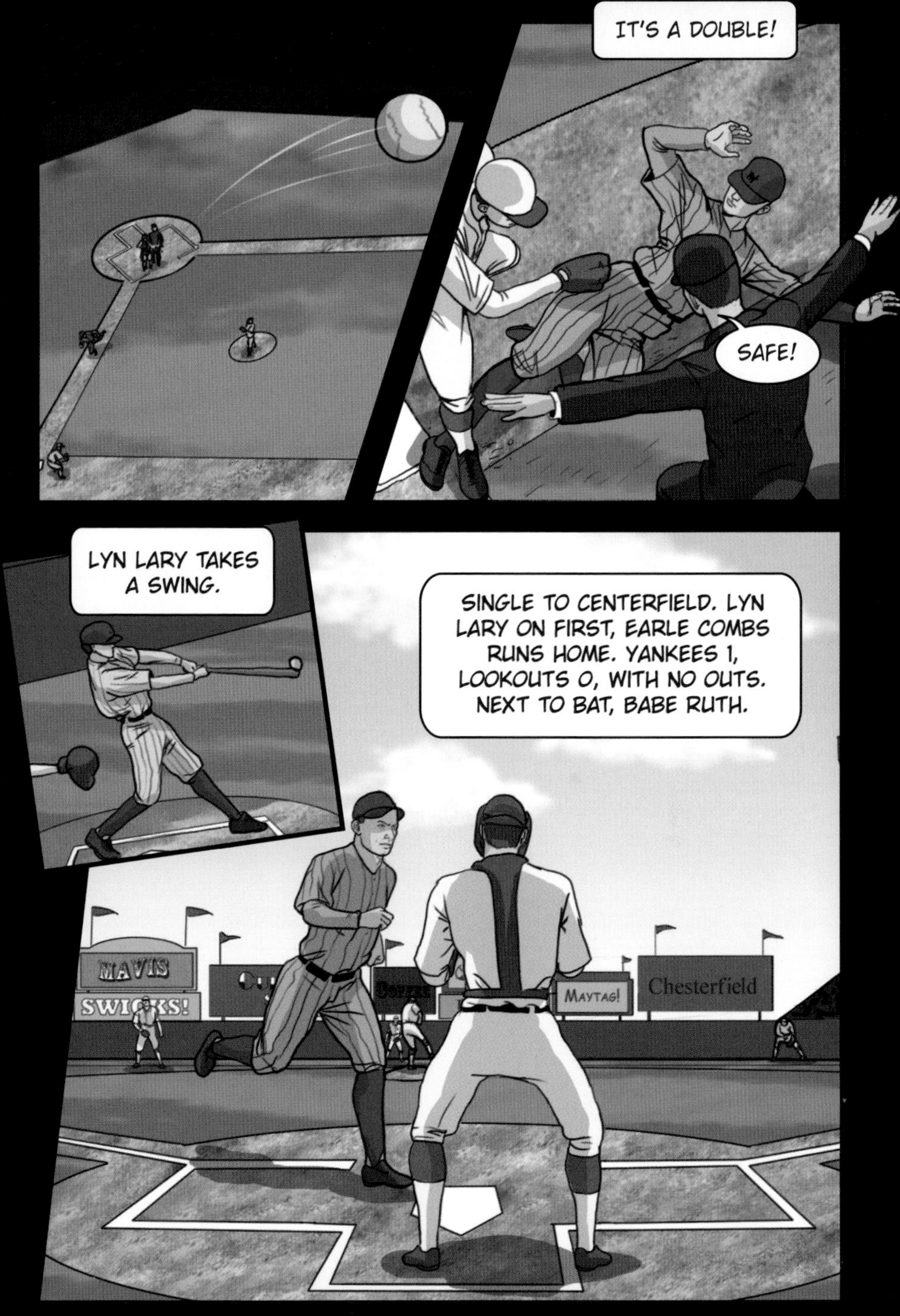
IT'S A DOUBLE!
SAFE!
LYN LARY TAKES A SWING.
SINGLE TO CENTERFIELD. LYN LARY ON FIRST, EARLE COMBS RUNS HOME. YANKEES 1, LOOKOUTS 0, WITH NO OUTS. NEXT TO BAT, BABE RUTH.
MAVIS
SWICKS!
MAYTAG!
Chesterfield

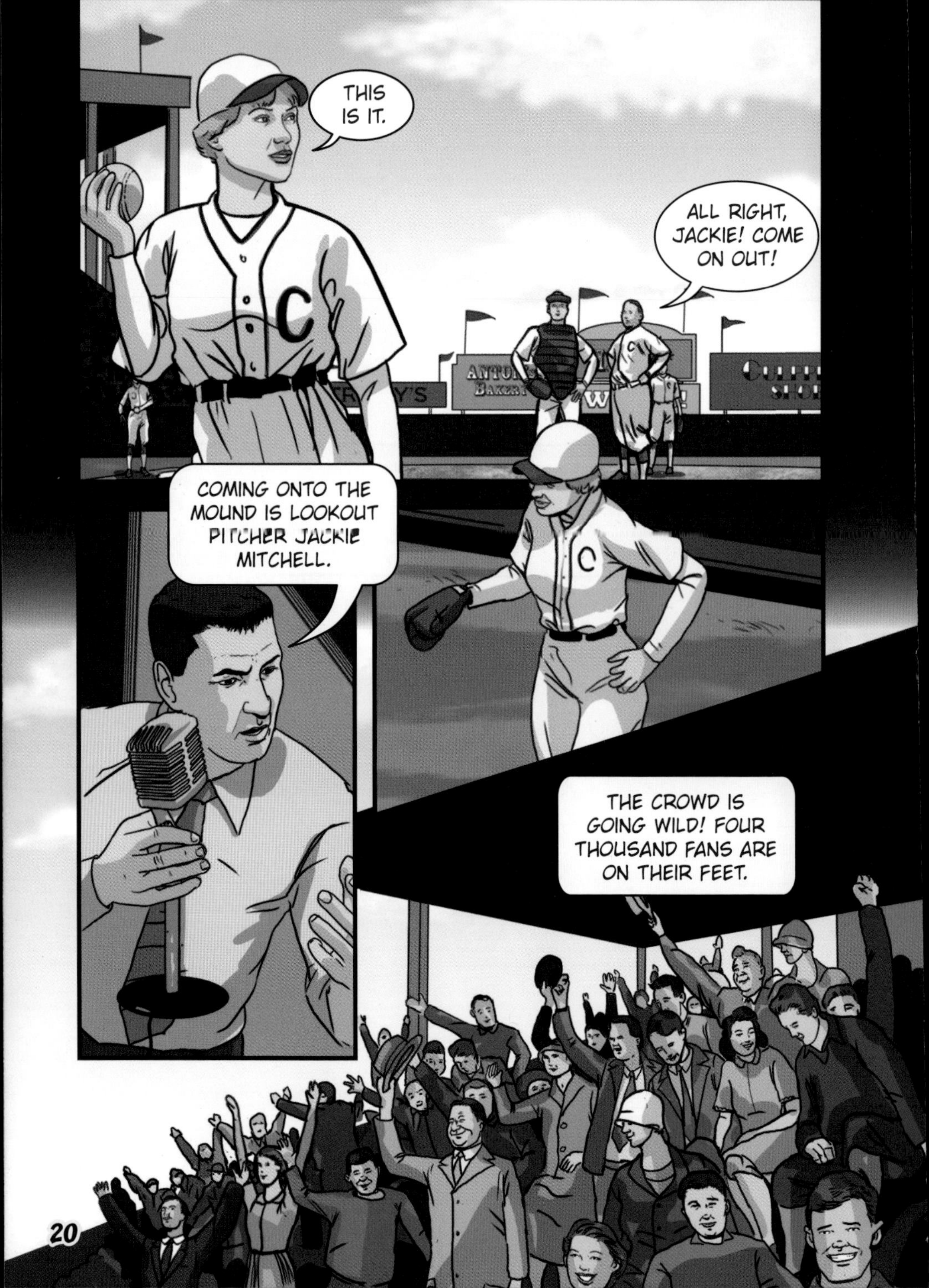
THIS IS IT.
ALL RIGHT, JACKIE! COME ON OUT!
COMING ONTO THE MOUND IS LOOKOUT PITCHER JACKIE MITCHELL.
THE CROWD IS GOING WILD! FOUR THOUSAND FANS ARE ON THEIR FEET.

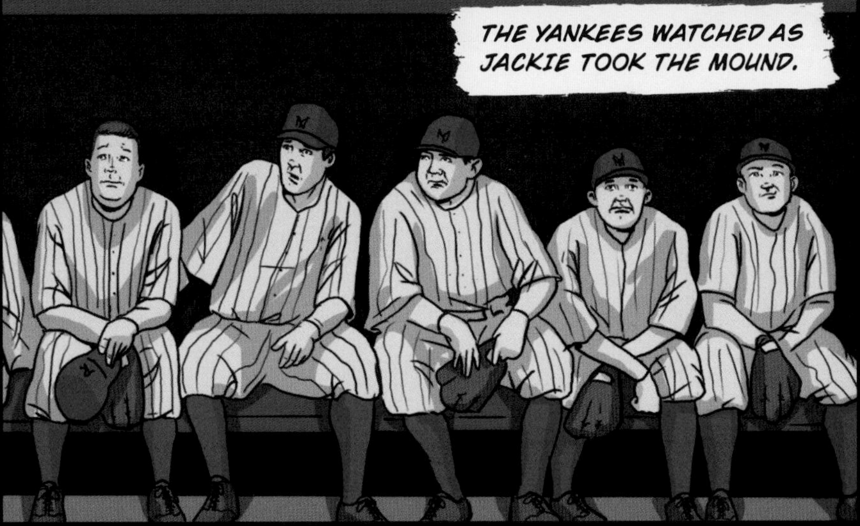
THE YANKEES WATCHED AS
JACKIE TOOK THE MOUND.

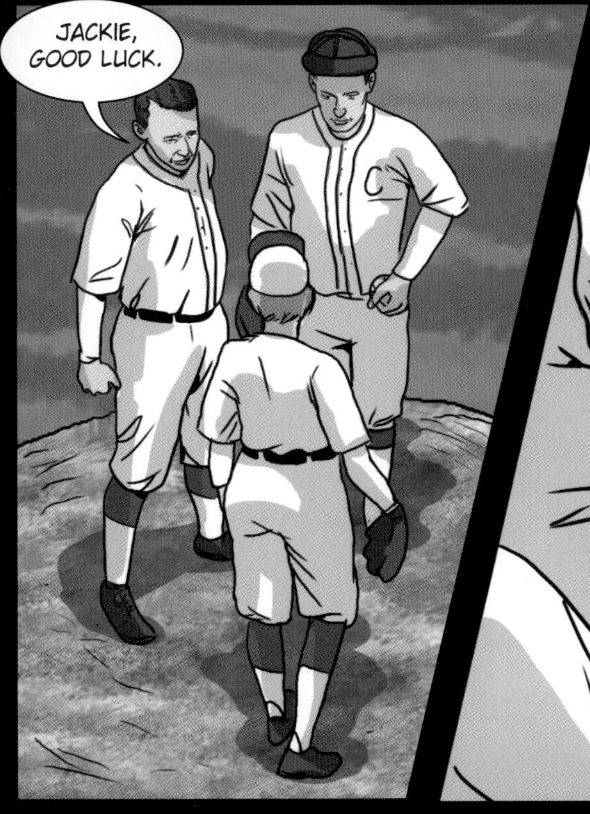
JACKIE,
GOOD LUCK.

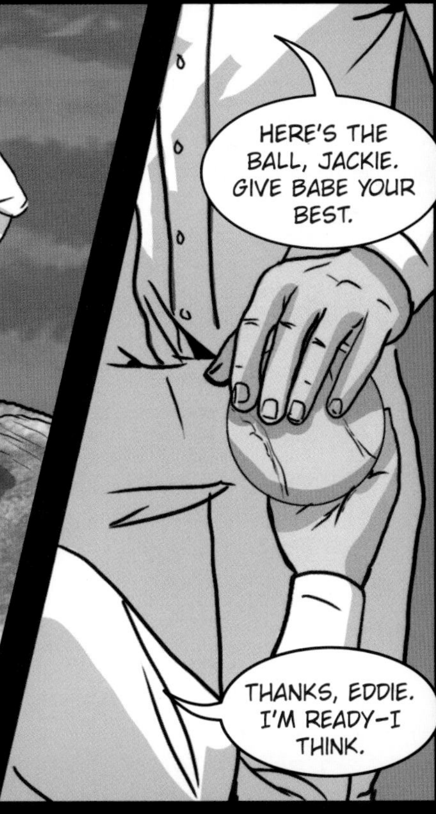
HERE'S THE BALL, JACKIE. GIVE BABE YOUR BEST.
THANKS, EDDIE. I'M READY—I THINK.

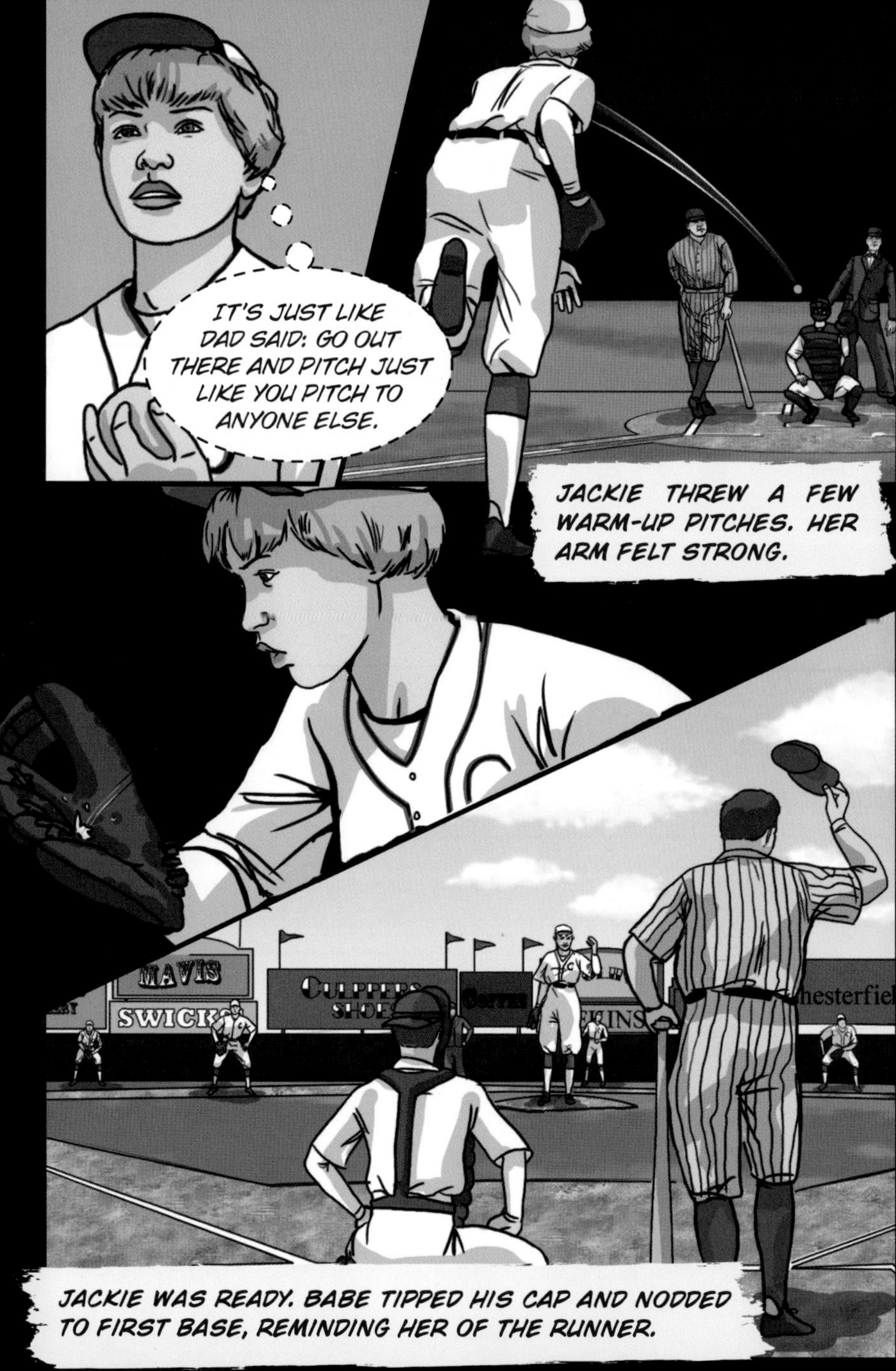
IT'S JUST LIKE DAD SAID: GO OUT THERE AND PITCH JUST LIKE YOU PITCH TO ANYONE ELSE.
JACKIE THREW A FEW WARM-UP PITCHES. HER ARM FELT STRONG.
MAVIS
SWICK
CULPPERS SHOES
COFFEE
hesterfiel
JACKIE WAS READY. BABE TIPPED HIS CAP AND NODDED TO FIRST BASE, REMINDING HER OF THE RUNNER.

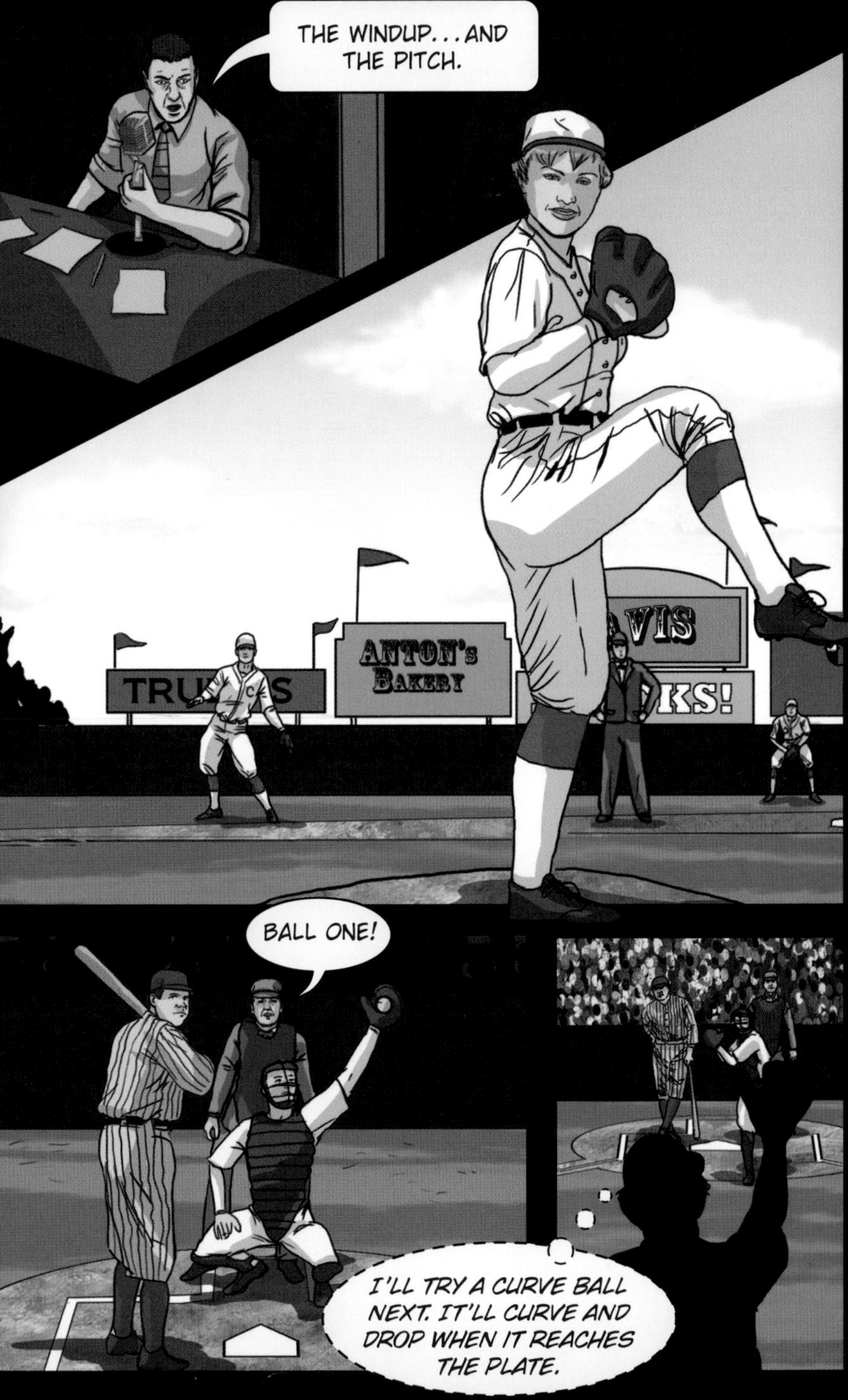
THE WINDUP... AND THE PITCH.
ANTON's BAKERY
BALL ONE!
I'LL TRY A CURVE BALL NEXT. IT'LL CURVE AND DROP WHEN IT REACHES THE PLATE.

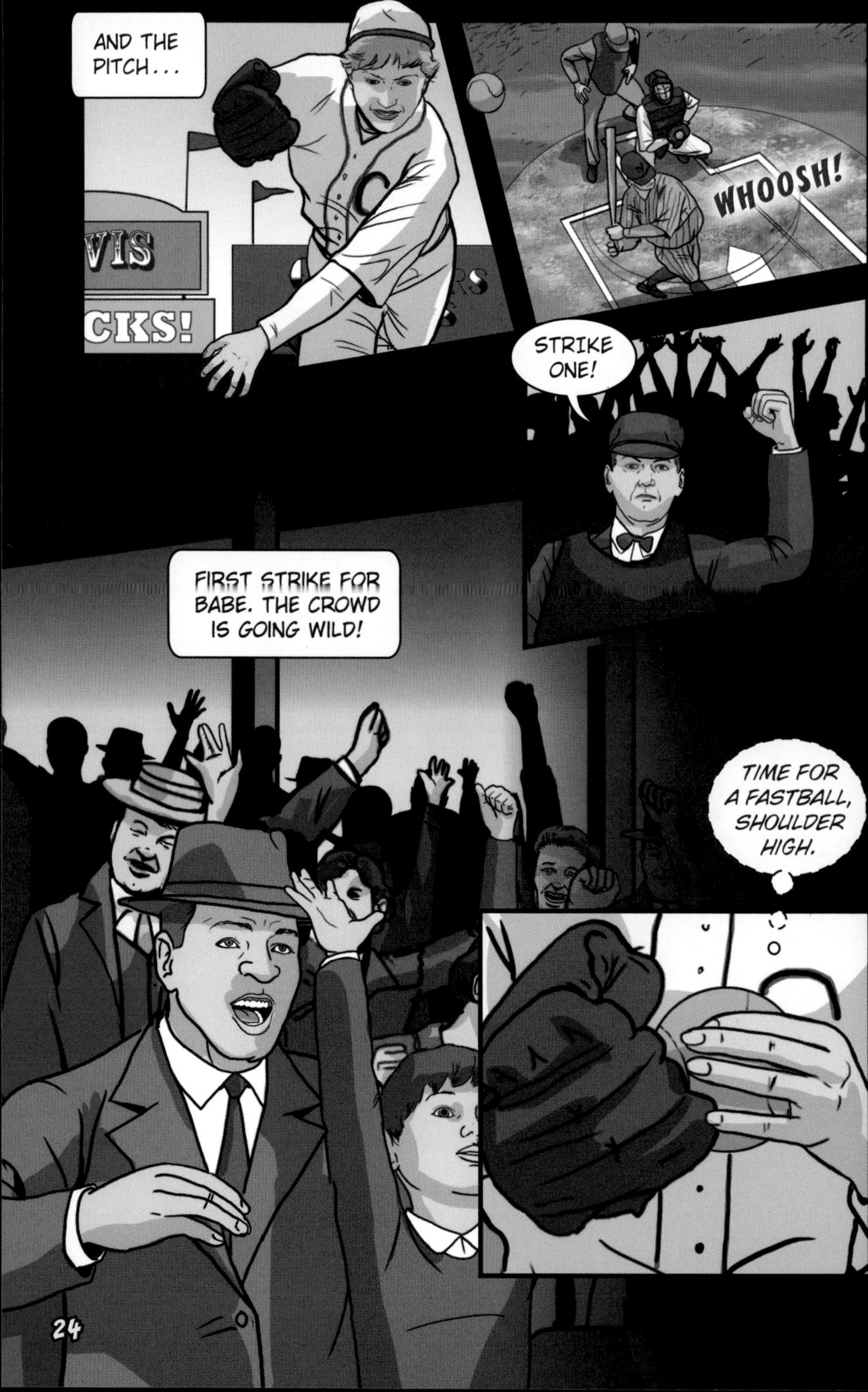
AND THE PITCH...
WHOOSH!
STRIKE ONE!
FIRST STRIKE FOR BABE. THE CROWD IS GOING WILD!
TIME FOR A FASTBALL, SHOULDER HIGH.

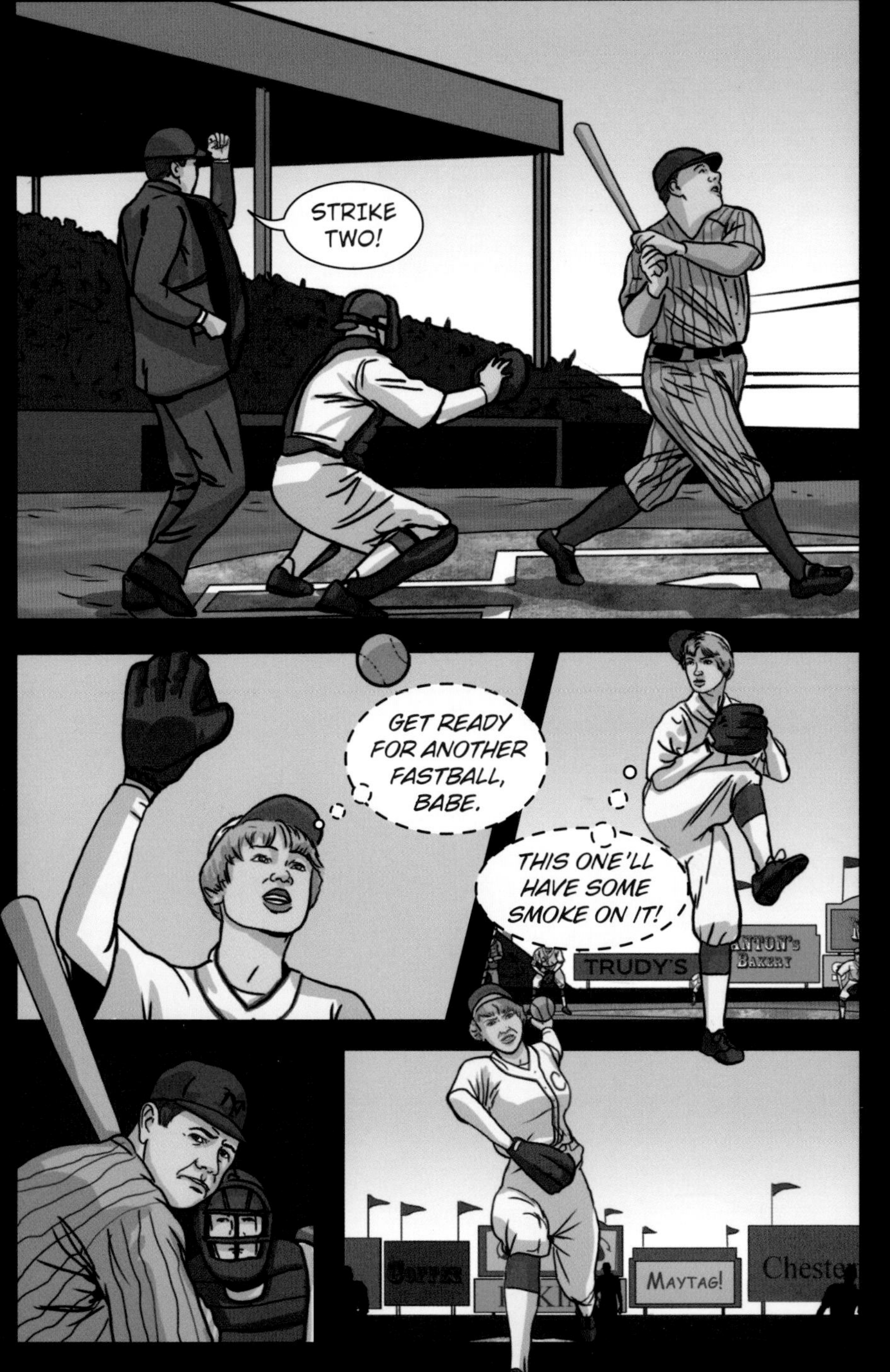
STRIKE TWO!
GET READY FOR ANOTHER FASTBALL, BABE.
THIS ONE'LL HAVE SOME SMOKE ON IT!
TRUDY'S
BAKERY
MAYTAG!
Chester

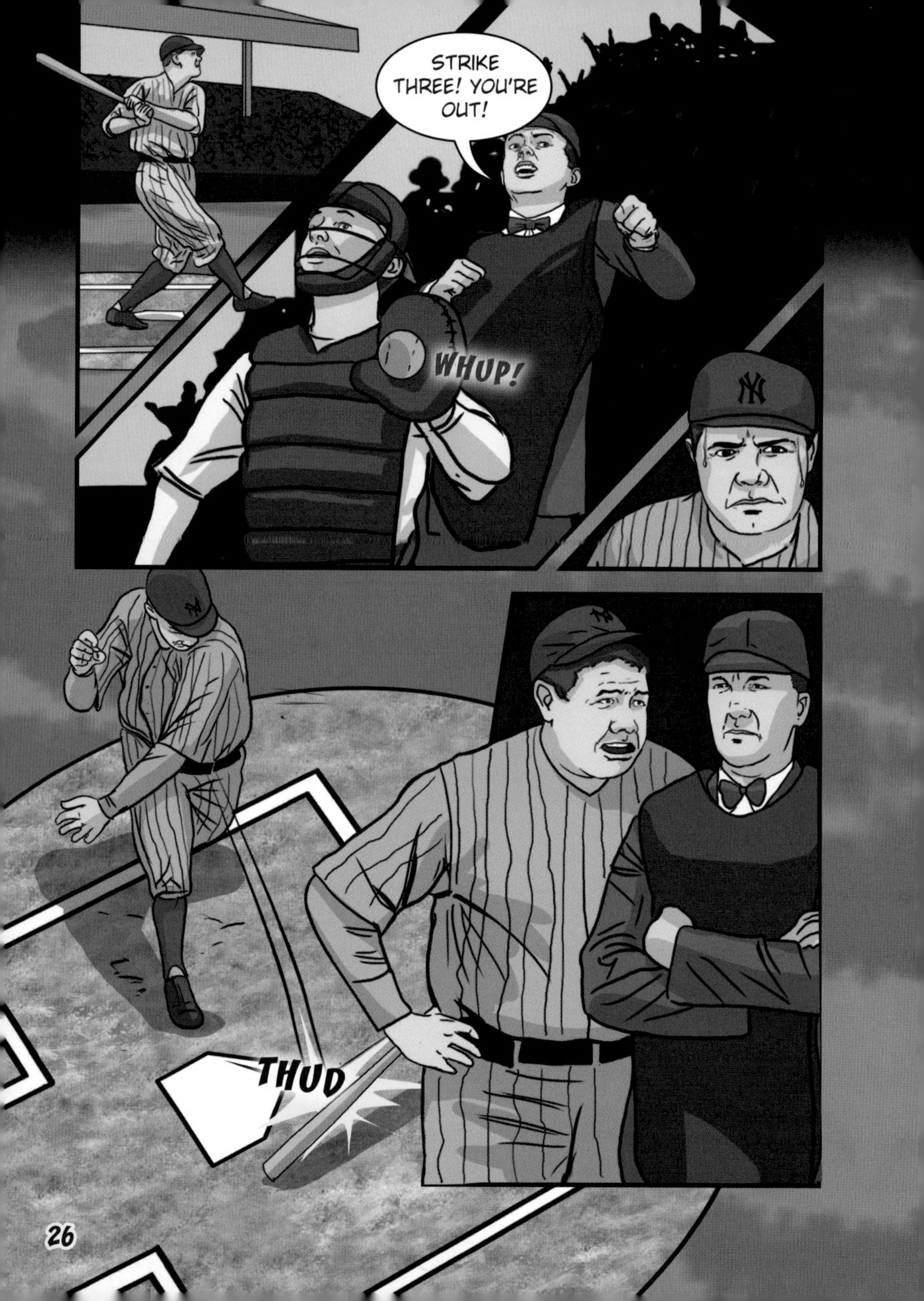
STRIKE THREE! YOU'RE OUT!
WHUP!
THUD

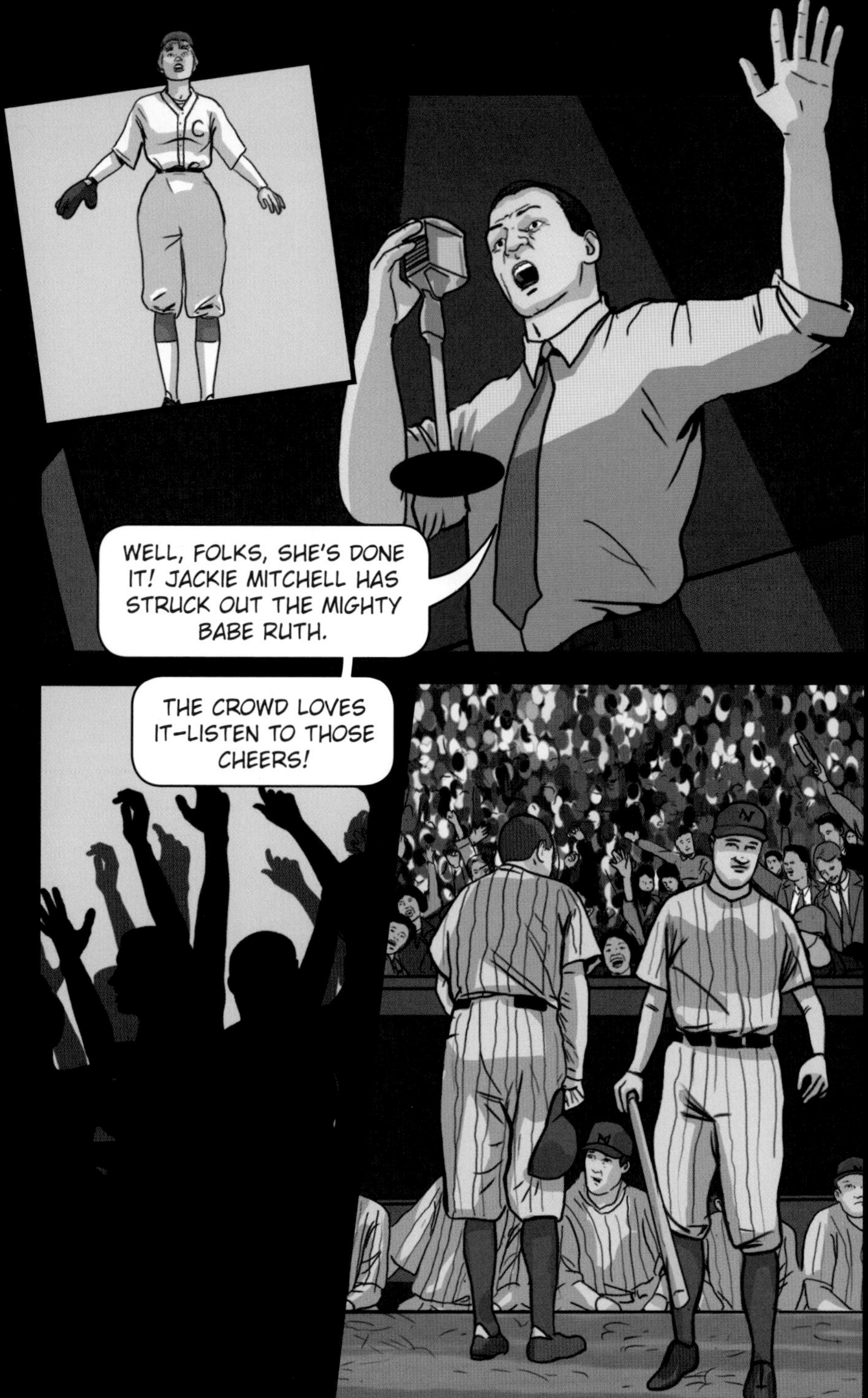
WELL, FOLKS, SHE'S DONE IT! JACKIE MITCHELL HAS STRUCK OUT THE MIGHTY BABE RUTH.
THE CROWD LOVES IT—LISTEN TO THOSE CHEERS!

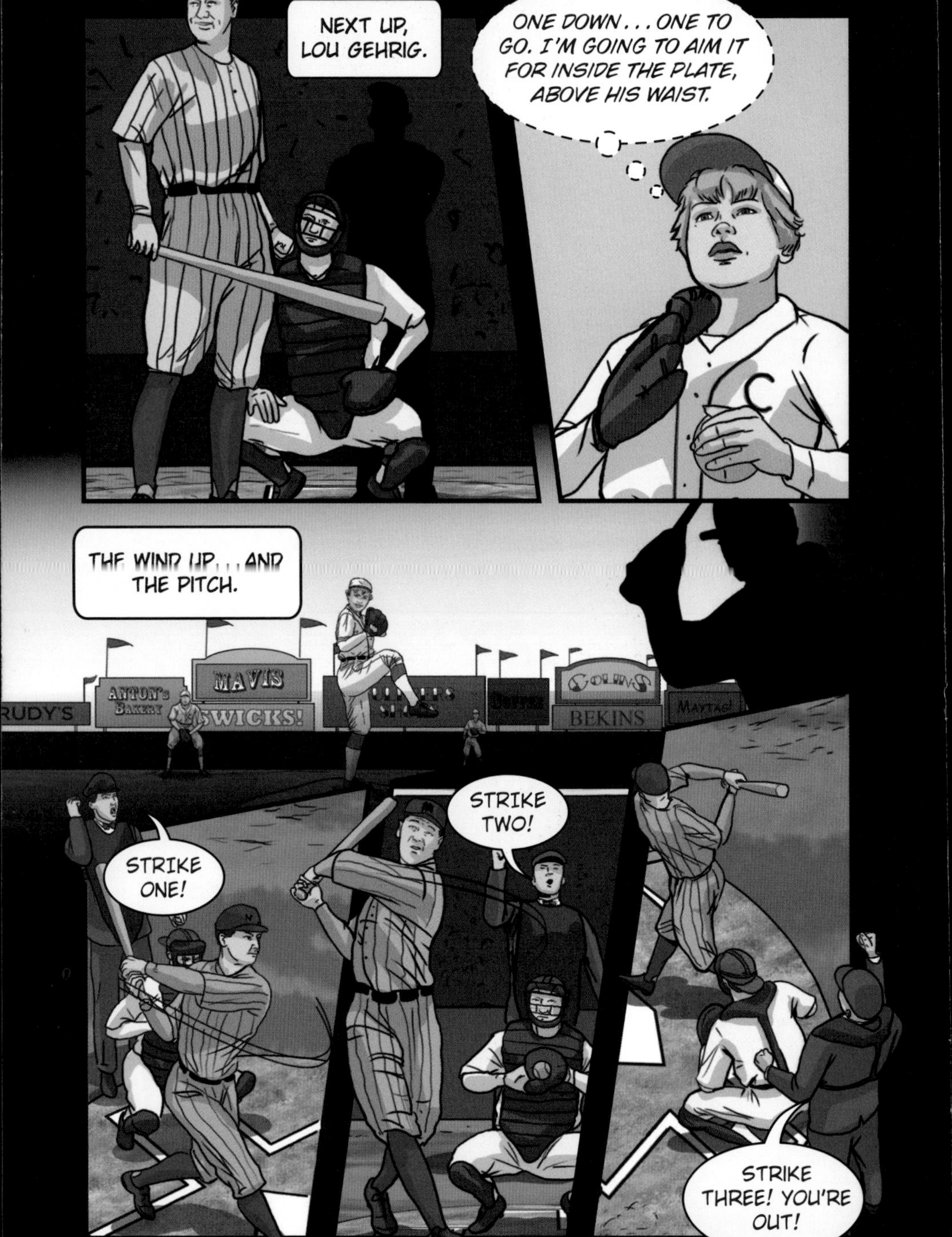

NEXT UP, LOU GEHRIG.
ONE DOWN . . . ONE TO GO. I'M GOING TO AIM IT FOR INSIDE THE PLATE, ABOVE HIS WAIST.
THE WIND UP . . . AND THE PITCH.
RUDY'S
ANTON'S BAKERY
MAVIS
SWICKS!
BEKINS
MAYTAG
STRIKE ONE!
STRIKE TWO!
STRIKE THREE! YOU'RE OUT!

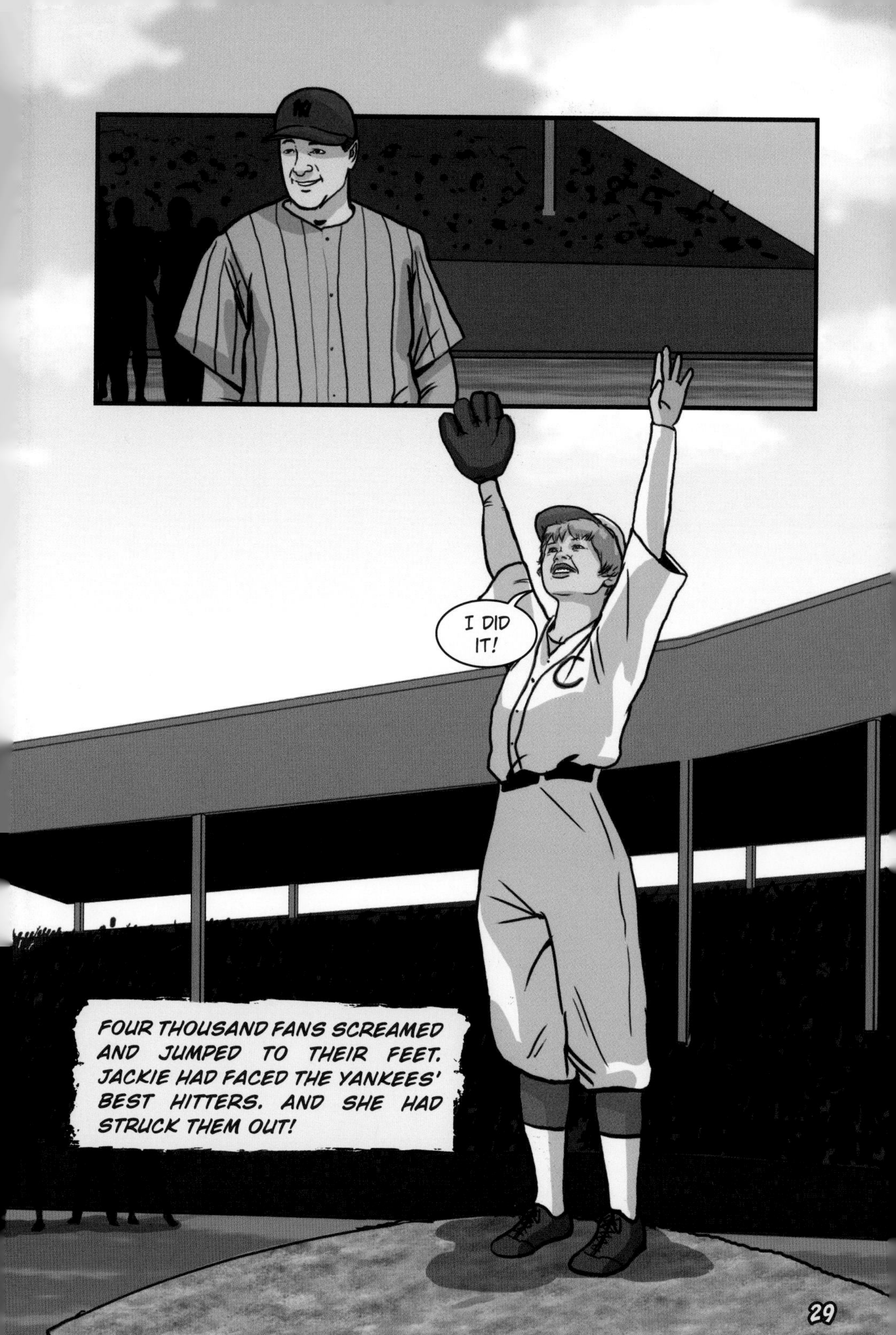
I DID IT!
FOUR THOUSAND FANS SCREAMED AND JUMPED TO THEIR FEET. JACKIE HAD FACED THE YANKEES' BEST HITTERS. AND SHE HAD STRUCK THEM OUT!

AFTERWORD

AFTER JACKIE STRUCK OUT RUTH AND GEHRIG, SHE WALKED TONY
LAZZERI. THEN MANAGER BERT NIEHOFF PULLED HER FROM THE GAME.
THE YANKEES WON 14-4. BUT THE NEXT DAY, JACKIE'S STORY WAS IN
NEWSPAPERS EVERYWHERE. JACKIE RECEIVED FAN MAIL FROM ALL OVER
THE COUNTRY.

KENESAW MOUNTAIN LANDIS, WHO WAS IN CHARGE OF PROFESSIONAL
BASEBALL, ALSO HEARD ABOUT THE STRIKEOUTS. LANDIS CANCELED
JACKIE'S CONTRACT AND BANNED HER FROM PROFESSIONAL BASEBALL.
HE BELIEVED THE GAME WAS TOO TOUGH FOR WOMEN. BUT JACKIE
CONTINUED TO PLAY BASEBALL INTO THE LATE 1930S.

JACKIE DIED IN 1987. BUT FANS STILL TALK ABOUT HER STRIKEOUTS.
SOME PEOPLE THINK THAT RUTH AND GEHRIG STRUCK OUT ON PURPOSE.
MAYBE JOE ENGEL PAID THEM TO DO IT, THEY SAY. AFTER ALL, ENGEL
WAS FAMOUS FOR HIS PUBLICITY STUNTS. OTHERS THINK THAT JACKIE
SURPRISED THE SLUGGERS. A DROP PITCH IS HARD FOR BATTERS TO
HIT, ESPECIALLY WHEN THEY ARE FACING A PITCHER FOR THE FIRST TIME.
AND IT WASN'T UNUSUAL FOR BABE RUTH TO STRIKE OUT. DURING HIS
CAREER, HE WHIFFED 1,330 TIMES!

JACKIE ALWAYS INSISTED THAT SHE STRUCK OUT
RUTH AND GEHRIG HONESTLY. THE DEBATE
WILL GO ON. BUT JACKIE MITCHELL WILL
ALWAYS BE REMEMBERED AS THE GIRL
WHO STRUCK OUT BABE RUTH.

FURTHER READING AND WEBSITES

AMERICA'S STORY FROM AMERICA'S LIBRARY: PLAY BALL!
HTTP://WWW.AMERICASLIBRARY.GOV/JP/BBALL/JP_BBALL_SUBJ.HTML

BOOTHROYD, JENNIFER. *LOU GEHRIG: A LIFE OF DEDICATION*.
MINNEAPOLIS: LERNER PUBLICATIONS COMPANY, 2008.

BURLEIGH, ROBERT. *HOME RUN: THE STORY OF BABE RUTH*. NEW YORK:
SANDPIPER, 2003.

KELLEY, JAMES E. *EYEWITNESS: BASEBALL*. NEW YORK: DK CHILDREN,
2005.

MACRAE, SLOAN. *THE NEW YORK YANKEES*. NEW YORK: POWERKIDS
PRESS, 2010.

MAJOR LEAGUE BASEBALL: KID'S DUGOUT
HTTP://MLB.MLB.COM/MLB/KIDS/INDEX.JSP

ROBERTS, RUSSELL. *100 BASEBALL LEGENDS WHO SHAPED SPORTS
HISTORY*. SAN FRANCISCO: BLUEWOOD BOOKS, 2003.

ROSEN, MICHAEL J. *BALLS! ROUND 2*. MINNEAPOLIS: MILLBROOK PRESS,
2008.

THE SCIENCE OF BASEBALL
HTTP://WWW.EXPLORATORIUM.EDU/BASEBALL/

STEWART, MARK, AND MIKE KENNEDY. *LONG BALL: THE LEGEND AND LORE
OF THE HOME RUN*. MINNEAPOLIS: MILLBROOK PRESS, 2006.

ABOUT THE AUTHOR

JEAN PATRICK EARNED DEGREES IN ENGLISH FROM LUTHER COLLEGE IN DECORAH, IOWA, AND KANSAS STATE UNIVERSITY IN MANHATTAN, KANSAS. SHE LIVES WITH HER FAMILY NEAR MITCHELL, SOUTH DAKOTA, WHERE SHE HAS MORE ANIMALS THAN SHE CAN COUNT, INCLUDING DOGS, CATS, COWS, HORSES, A COCKATIEL, AND A NOISY DONKEY NAMED CACTUS.

ABOUT THE ADAPTER

EMMA CARLSON BERNE HAS WRITTEN AND EDITED MORE THAN TWO DOZEN BOOKS FOR YOUNG PEOPLE, INCLUDING BIOGRAPHIES OF SUCH DIVERSE FIGURES AS CHRISTOPHER COLUMBUS, WILLIAM SHAKESPEARE, THE HILTON SISTERS, AND SNOOP DOGG. SHE HOLDS A MASTER'S DEGREE IN COMPOSITION AND RHETORIC FROM MIAMI UNIVERSITY. MS. BERNE LIVES IN CINCINNATI, OHIO, WITH HER HUSBAND AND SON.

ABOUT THE ILLUSTRATORS

TED HAMMOND IS A CANADIAN ARTIST, LIVING AND WORKING JUST OUTSIDE OF TORONTO. HAMMOND HAS CREATED ARTWORK FOR EVERYTHING FROM FANTASY AND COMIC-BOOK ART TO CHILDREN'S MAGAZINES, POSTERS, AND BOOK ILLUSTRATION.

RICHARD PIMENTEL CARBAJAL HAS A BROAD SPECTRUM OF ILLUSTRATIVE SPECIALTIES. HIS BACKGROUND HAS FOCUSED ON LARGE-SCALE INSTALLATIONS AND SCENERY. CARBAJAL RECENTLY HAS EXPANDED INTO THE BOOK PUBLISHING AND ADVERTISING MARKETS.

Text copyright © 2011 by Jean L. S. Patrick
Illustrations © 2011 by Lerner Publishing Group, Inc.

Graphic Universe™ is a trademark of Lerner Publishing Group, Inc.

Graphic Universe™
A division of Lerner Publishing Group, Inc.
241 First Avenue North
Minneapolis, MN 55401 U.S.A.

Website address: www.lernerbooks.com

Patrick, Jean L. S.
    The baseball adventure of Jackie Mitchell, girl pitcher vs. Babe Ruth / by Jean L. S. Patrick ; adapted by Emma Carlson Berne ; illustrated by Ted Hammond and Richard Carbajal.
        p.   cm. — (History's kid heroes)
    Includes bibliographical references.
        ISBN: 978-0-7613-6180-0 (lib. bdg. : alk. paper)   1. Mitchell, Jackie, 1914–1987—Juvenile literature.   2. Ruth, Babe, 1895–1948—Juvenile literature.   3. Gehrig, Lou, 1903–1941—Juvenile literature.   4. Baseball—Comic books, strips, etc.   5. Graphic novels.   I. Berne, Emma Carlson. II. Hammond, Ted.   III. Carbajal, Richard.   IV. Title.
GV867.5.P37 2011
796.357092—dc22
    [B]   2010028951

Manufactured in the United States of America
1—CG—12/31/10